KU-759-760

Heinemann
New Windmills

STONE COLD

Desperate to escape from his brutish stepfather, Link leaves
his home in Bradford and travels to London. His hopes for a
new beginning are soon shattered, however, when his
money runs out and he finds himself homeless, alone and
frightened on the cold streets of London.

When Link meets the streetwise Ginger he feels that
things are beginning to look up, as he learns the tricks of survival. But even their friendship is no protection from the
sinister threat that is creeping up on them and all the homeless of London, intent on a deadly mission . . .

ABOUT THE AUTHOR

Robert Swindells was born in Bradford in 1939. He left
school at 15 and worked for a local newspaper before join-
ing the RAF for three years. He then had a variety of jobs,
including shop assistant, clerk, printer and engineer. In 1969
he started training to be a teacher. He taught for eight years
before becoming a full-time writer.

Of his writing, Robert Swindells comments:

*I am dedicated to the idea that we are all responsible for one
another, and that we ought to conduct ourselves accord-
ingly, doing no harm to any being. My work reflects this
belief.*

At the age of 50, he spent three nights living rough in North
London, to form an understanding of day-to-day life on the
streets.

He now lives on the Yorkshire Moors with his wife
Brenda.

ROBERT SWINDELLS

STONE COLD

Carnegie Medal Winner

Heinemann
New Windmills

Heinemann Educational Publishers
Halley Court, Jordan Hill, Oxford OX2 8EJ
a division of Reed Educational & Professional Publishing Ltd

OXFORD   MELBOURNE   AUCKLAND
JOHANNESBURG   BLANTYRE   GABORONE
IBADAN   PORTSMOUTH (NH) USA   CHICAGO

09 08 07 06 05 04 03
20 19 18 17 16 15

ISBN 0 435 12468 4

Cover illustration by Paul Hunt
Cover design by The Point
Typeset by Books Unlimited (Nottm) NG19 7QZ
Printed and bound in the United Kingdom by Clays Ltd, St Ives plc

In memory of Bob Cryer, M.P.
There was room in his *world for all of us*

You can call me Link. It's not my name, but it's what I say when anybody asks, which isn't often. I'm invisible, see? One of the invisible people. Right now I'm sitting in a doorway watching the passers-by. They avoid looking at me. They're afraid I want something they've got, and they're right. Also, they don't want to think about me. They don't like reminding I exist. Me, and those like me. We're living proof that everything's not all right and we make the place untidy.

Hang about and I'll tell you the story of my fascinating life.

Shelter. Yes. I like it. It's got a ring to it as I'm sure you'll agree. Shelter, as in shelter from the stormy blast. It's what they're all seeking. The street people. What they crave. If they can only find shelter everything will be fine. Well – get fell in, my lucky lads. I'm ready for you.

My fascinating life.

Yes.

Born March 20th, 1977, in Bradford, Yorkshire to Mr & Mrs X. We were a family, you know – as happy as most, till Dad ran off with a receptionist in 1991, when I was fourteen and at the local comp. This mucked up my school work for quite a while, but that's not why I ended up like this. No. Vincent's to blame for that. Good old Vince. Mum's boyfriend. You should see him. I mean, Mum's no Kylie Minogue – but Vincent. He's about fifty for a start, and he's one of these old dudes that wear cool gear and try to act young and it doesn't work because they've got grey hair and fat bellies and they just make themselves pathetic. And as if that's not enough, Vince likes his ale. I suppose Dad must've been a bit of a bastard in his way, but at least he wasn't a boozer. You should see the state Vincent's in when he and Mum come home from the club. He's got this very loud laugh – laughing at nothing, if you know what I mean – and he stands there with his arm round Mum, slurring his words as he tells me to call him Dad. Dad. I wouldn't call that fat pillock Dad if he was the last guy on earth. And the one thing that really bugs me is the way he leers at Mum and comes out with this very suggestive stuff about going to bed and rounding off a decent night. In all the years Dad was with us, I never once knew him to mention sex in my hearing, or even hint at it. This slob leers and winks and nudges with

3

one eye on me to see how I'm taking it, and Mum just laughs and shoves him and says ooh, you are a one. It makes me puke.

He's changed her. That's one of the things I hate him for. She used to be one of those quiet people who are satisfied with the daily routine of their lives. She hardly ever went out at night – she didn't seem to want to. She was wrapped up in her family, I guess. She was always there when you needed her and I think she loved us. Me and Carole, I mean.

Oh, I know how it sounds, me going on like this about Mum as though she wasn't entitled to a life of her own. Of course she's entitled, but what I'm saying is, why Vince?

Carole's my sister, by the way. She's four years older than me and she always spoiled me, and when good old Vince moved in and Mum started changing it was Carole who made life bearable for me. It was bad, but I could stand it with her there to support me. Then one night when Mum was working late, something happened between Carole and Vince. I didn't understand it then and she never told me anything, but I've a fair idea now what it must've been. Anyway, she said something to Mum and they had this flaming row and it ended with Carole walking out of the house. She moved in with her boyfriend and I was on my own. I stuck it out till I finished school, but that was it. I'd got five GCSEs, which was a miracle when you remember what was going on at home, but I couldn't get a job and there's no government money for school-leavers. You're supposed to be on a training scheme, but there aren't enough places and I didn't get one. I'm sure Mum would've supported me till I found something, but it wasn't long before Vince started on at me about living on his money. I wasn't living on his money – I'd have topped myself first. It was Mum's money, but he went on and on, getting nastier and nastier, and one night when I'd been with my mates he locked me out of the house. It wasn't even his house but he locked the door and wouldn't let Mum open it. I went round to Carole's and she let me spend the night, and when I got home next morning Vince started slapping me around the head for going off and worrying Mum. If you happen to know anybody who's looking for a one hundred per cent out-and-out bastard, I can let him have Vince's address.

Anyway, that's how he was with me and I guess Mum's scared of him because she didn't stick up for me, so I left. You'd have left too, in my place. Anybody would. It's called making yourself homeless. And so here I am sitting in this doorway which is now my bedroom, hoping some kind punter will give me a bit of small change so I can eat.

Good, eh?

I'm getting used to my name. Breaking it in like a pair of new boots. Good morning, Shelter, I say to the bathroom mirror. Smiling. Good morning, Shelter. You're a handsome devil but you're idle, lad. You need a shave. I've been writing it, too, on the backs of old envelopes. Shelter. Shelter. Shelter. It's starting to look like an authentic signature already. I realize of course that all this has precious little to do with recruiting, and perhaps you think I'm stalling. Putting it off.

Not so. I'm merely indulging myself. After all there's plenty of time. The street people aren't going to go away, and anticipation is the best part of a treat, as my old grannie never used to say. So it's a case of wait for it, you 'orrible little man.

I didn't come to London straightaway. I may be homeless and unemployed but I'm not stupid. I'd read about London. I knew the streets down here weren't paved with gold. I knew there were hundreds of people – thousands, in fact – sleeping rough and begging for coppers. But that's just the point, see? In Bradford I stuck out like a sore thumb because there weren't many of us. The police down here have got used to seeing kids kipping in doorways, and mostly they leave you alone. In Bradford I was getting moved on every hour or so. I was getting no sleep at all, and practically no money. People up there haven't got used to beggars yet. They're embarrassed. They'll make large detours to avoid passing close to you, and if somebody does come within earshot and you ask for change, they look startled and hurry on by.

Also, I kept seeing people I knew. Neighbours. Guys I'd been at school with. I even saw one of my teachers once. And if you've never been caught begging by someone who knew you before, you can't possibly know how low it makes you feel.

I wasn't out every night, back then. That was the one good thing about it. Once or twice a week I'd show up at my sister's for a bath, a meal and a decent night's sleep. Trouble was, I was getting scruffier and scruffier, which happens if you sleep in your clothes, and Chris, Carole's feller, got resentful of my visits. He didn't actually say anything to me, but I could see it in his eyes and hear it in his tone of voice, and I knew Carole must be catching hell from him every time I'd been there. So, what with one thing and another, I decided it was time to move on.

Sounds good, right? Time to move on. Reminds you of all those old songs about the restless character who hates to stay too long in one place. He meets a girl who falls in love with him, but after a while he hears the old highway calling and so he slings his bed-roll over his shoulder and moves on, leaving the girl to grieve. Dead romantic, eh?

Forget it. Sad, is what it is. Sad and scary. You're leaving a place you know and heading into the unknown with nothing to protect you. No money. No prospect of work. No address where folks will make you welcome. You're going to find yourself living among hard, violent people, some of whom are deranged. You're going to be at risk every minute, day and night. Especially night. There are guys so desperate or so crazy, they'll knife you or batter your head in for your sleeping-bag and the coppers you've got in your pocket. There are some who'll try to get in your sleeping-bag with you, because you're a nice-looking lad with soft skin and no stubble. And there's nowhere you can run to, because nobody cares. Nobody gives a damn. You're just another dosser, and one dosser more or less makes no difference.

I've been out tonight. I took the tube down to Charing Cross and walked about a bit. Tour of inspection, you might say. And I found them, as I'd known I would. Hundreds of the scruffy blighters, lying around making the place look manky. I marched along the Strand and there they were, dossing in all the doorways – even Lloyds Bank and the Law Courts. One cheeky little bugger – couldn't have been more than seventeen – actually asked me for money. Have you got any change, he says. I looked him up and down and I said, 'Change? I'd change you, my lad, if I had you in khaki for six weeks.' It didn't go in, though. He just smiled and said have a nice night. Cracker up his arse, that's what he wants. That'd wake him up. That, or six weeks at Strensall.

National Service. That was the thing. It brought 'em all in – the teds, the rockers, the Mammy's boys. And it changed 'em, by golly it did. In six weeks. There were no teddy boys on that passing-out parade I can tell you, and no rockers, either. Soldiers, that's what it made of 'em. There were no exceptions.

And that was my mission in life – to turn dirty, scruffy, pimply youths into soldiers. Into men. And I did it, too. Year after year.

Yes, and what thanks do I get? I'll tell you. They chuck me out. Twenty-nine years' service and they turn round and chuck me out. Medical grounds, it says on the chit. Discharged on medical grounds. And there's nothing wrong with me. Nothing. I'm forty-seven and fit as a butcher's dog.

Medical grounds is just an excuse, of course. I know why they really chucked me out. They chucked me out because their mission in life is exactly the opposite of mine. They think I don't know that, but I do. They're all part of the plot, see? There's a plot – it's been hatching a long time now – to undermine the country by clogging it up with dossers and junkies and drunks. Some of the top politicians are in it, and civil servants and social workers and even the church. They want to flood the country with winos and crims and down-and-outs and drag it down till it's no better than some of the filthy holes I've served in all these years. They're powerful, and they'll stop at nothing. What's the career of one Sergeant-Major to them? Nothing, that's what. Nothing.

They're not going to stop me, though. Oh, no. They abolished National Service, and they've put me where I can't turn garbage into men anymore, but I can clean up the garbage, can't I? They can't stop me doing that, and I will. By golly I will.

Now – where did we get to? Oh, yes – I remember. Time to move on.

I'd applied for loads of jobs in the months since I'd left school. Office work. Supermarkets. Catering. Filling stations – you name it. Most employers wanted experience, and some ads actually said unemployed persons need not apply, which is criminal, in my opinion. I'd started applying in August and I'd had a couple of interviews, but as I said before, sleeping in your clothes makes you look scruffy, and by Christmas I looked like a tramp. I knew nobody was going to take me on looking like that, and I started getting really depressed.

Christmas didn't help. I spent it at Carole's, which was kind of her and Chris, but it was still the worst Christmas I'd ever had. For a start, there was my present. Carole and Mum had put their money together and got me this sleeping-bag. A really posh job. Quilted, waterproof, the lot. It must have cost a bomb and I knew they only meant to be kind, but it said something to me. It said they thought of me as a dosser – as someone who might always be a dosser, so he might as well be as comfy as possible. It hurt like hell, but I didn't let them see. And I've got to admit it's come in handy ever since.

Anyway, there was that, and then there was Boxing Day. Boxing Day Mum came round, and she brought Vince with her. I can only think that Carole had never

11

told Chris the full story about him, or surely Chris wouldn't have had him in the house. Anyway, they came for dinner and stayed till one o'clock next morning, and of course everybody got drunk. Everybody except me. And once he got a skinful, Vince started making cracks about me. The ghost of Christmas past, he called me. Don't ask me why. I was a disgrace, he said, stuffing myself with my sister's grub. Sitting there with my long hair and tatty clothes, making Mum feel guilty when she'd had nothing to feel guilty about. I was a scrounger, a sponger and a layabout, and I ought to be looking for work instead of sitting with a face as long as a fiddle, spoiling everybody's Christmas.

It didn't feel like peace on earth, I can tell you that. There wasn't a lot of goodwill toward men floating about. And the worst thing was, nobody stuck up for me. Not even my sister. It was then I knew I'd worn out my welcome, even here. So.

On December 28th I borrowed the price of a one-way ticket to London. Carole lent me the money. She even came to see me off at the station, and hugged me before I climbed on board with my backpack and my bed-roll. The next hug I got was from a stinky old ciderhead in Lincoln's Inn Fields when I gave him twenty pence so he'd leave me alone.

It is 19.00 hours and this has been a most satisfactory day. Most satisfactory. The secret of victory in any campaign is planning and preparation. My planning has been meticulous, and my preparations are now complete.

I have acquired a cat. This was my finishing touch. I can't abide the arse-licking, hair-scattering beasts myself, but you have to admit there's something reassuring about a home with a cat in it. A cat speaks of warmth, comfort, placid domesticity. A man who keeps a cat can't possibly mean anybody harm, can he?

I've christened it Sappho. A brilliant touch this, suggesting as it does a degree of scholarship in the creature's owner. I don't even know whether the bloody thing's male or female and I don't care – the point being is that a feller with a cat called Sappho is going to project a certain sort of image. Kindly and a bit academic. He might be expected to have a vague conscience about sleeping snug and warm while others live rough. He'll be a bumbler, but he might be stirred now and then to actually do something about this – to offer grub and a bed for the night to some poor unfortunate soul, no strings attached.

So it's Shelter and Sappho. Could be a series on the telly, couldn't it? Shelter and Sappho, otherwise known as The Invincibles. All is ready. Recruiting can now commence.

So London it was and London it is.

I made loads of mistakes. Most people do, first time in London. Trouble is, once you've made them it's practically impossible to put things right – you're on the old downward spiral and that's that. I know you've no idea what I'm on about, so listen.

I arrived in midwinter. Not a good idea. Okay, so things were bad at home. Really bad, and I had to get out. But if I'd known what I know now, I'd have hung in there a bit longer – toughed it out with Carole and Chris till March or even April. Spend one January night in a shop doorway and you'll know why.

I had a hundred and fifty quid on me when I got off the train at King's Cross. It was what was left of my savings, plus a twenty Carole slipped me when Chris wasn't looking. A hundred and fifty. Doesn't sound bad, does it? It sounded okay to me. My plan was, I'd get a room somewhere. Nothing posh. A bedsit, and then I'd look for work. Again, nothing posh. I'd take anything for a start, just till I established myself and could look round properly. I was dead green, see? A babe in arms. It isn't like that, but I didn't know.

I strode out of the station with my backpack and bedroll, and it felt like a new beginning. This was London, wasn't it? The centre, where it all happens. It's big, it's fast, and it's full of opportunities. Nobody knows you. Where you're from and what's gone before – that's your business. All that stuff with Vince – it never happened. It's a clean sheet – you can invent your own past and call yourself anything you choose.

I made a brilliant start, or so it seemed at the time. I turned right out of the station and started walking. I'd no idea where I was going. I was looking for somewhere to live. The street I was walking up was called Pancras Road. I hadn't gone far when I came to this row of shops under a block of flats. One was a newsagent's, and there were some postcards stuck on the glass door. I went for a closer look. They were ads, as I'd thought they'd be. Articles for sale. Babysitter wanted. House repairs done cheap. One said 'B&B, suit working man, rent negotiable.' The word negotiable was spelt 'Negoshable', and the whole thing looked like a six-year-old had written it, but I didn't care. There was an address. Wharfedale Road. I went in the shop and asked directions, and it was back the way I'd come.

It was a sleazoid place, and the rent wasn't all that negoshable either. 'Fifty a week,' the guy said. He'd a face like a rat. 'Fortnight in advance,' he said, 'and I'm doing you a favour. Most places want a month.'

'I'm looking for work,' I told him. 'I haven't much money. Can we negotiate?' (I told you I was green.)

'Negotiate?' His voice was a sort of screech. 'You can negotiate yourself right out of my house, lad, if that's your attitude. It's fifty a week, take it or leave it.'

I took it, and that was my second mistake. Oh, I was thankful at the time, don't think I wasn't. I'd a place to lay my head and keep out of the weather, and I hadn't been in London an hour. If I'd known, though, there were other places I could have tried – places like the YMCA, where there's help and advice and food as well as a bed if you're lucky enough to get in. But like I said, I didn't know.

I looked for work. I really did. First thing next morning I went to the Job Centre. The woman there said I should go to the Careers Office because I wasn't eighteen. She said I should go to the DSS as well. I went to the Careers Office and filled in a form. They asked where I'd come from and I said the north. I didn't want to be too precise in case good old Vince took it into his head to come looking for me. I gave them my new address but it was just like at home – there was no work, and no training places. I went to the DSS and filled in another form. I asked for advice and a guy interviewed me. I told him I had fifty pounds after paying two weeks' rent in advance, and that I was looking for work. He asked me a lot of stuff about why I'd left home. I explained about Vince and Chris and all that, and he said they'd have to decide whether I was entitled to anything. It might be several weeks, he said.

That was when I started to feel nervous. I had a room for two weeks, maximum. I didn't know much, but I'd a feeling rat-face wasn't the sort who'd wait for his money. If I wasn't earning within a fortnight I'd be out on my ear.

Daily Routine Orders 5

It's begun, the recruiting, and it was easy as falling off a log. I didn't even have to go far. My flat – mine and Sappho's – is in Mornington Place, and I found my first recruit in a doorway near Camden Station. A mile, if that. Mind you, it was a filthy night. Cold, wet and windy. Cut straight through you, that wind. I was wearing a parka, stormproof overtrousers and strong boots and I was still perished. What he must have felt like in damp, tatty denim I shudder to think. It was 01.30 so he'd probably been there an hour or two, freezing his tabs off, and that's why he came so easy.

What I did was, I squatted down in front of him and said, 'What's up mate – down on your luck?' I smiled as I said this – my best do-gooder smile. I was prepared for a possible rebuff. I mean, he might have been deeply suspicious – thought I was a woofta or something – but it didn't seem to cross his mind. Half daft with cold, probably. Anyway, he opened his eyes and looked at me and frowned and mumbled, 'Who are you?'

He was Scottish.

'Me?' I gave him a smile again. 'Shelter's my name. I help run the hostel on Plender Street.'

That got him. 'Hostel?' he says. 'What sort of hostel?'

'For young people,' I said. 'The Townhouse Project. You might have heard of us.' He wouldn't because we didn't exist. I'd made the whole thing up – name and everything. Part of my preparation.

He fell for it. Hook, line and sinker. 'Any chance of a bed?' he says. 'Bite to eat?' I shook my head – the rueful gesture I'd practised in the mirror. 'Not tonight, I'm afraid. Full up. Might be something tomorrow if you get there early.'

'Ah,' he says, and the light goes out of his eyes. He's thinking about the long cold hours ahead.

I let him ponder the prospect for a bit, then said, casual like, 'There's a comfy couch at my place if you don't mind roughing it.' Roughing it. Brilliant touch, that, and it worked.

'You sure?' he says. The light's back, and I can see his little brain working. He's thinking, this guy runs a hostel. Warm beds. Grub. It gets full, but if I'm with him I'm in, right? 'You sure?' he says. I gave him the smile again. 'Sure. No prob. It's just round the corner. Come on.'

And that's all there was to it. I strode out and he trotted at my heels like a ruddy poodle. It was pissing it down and he was sodden by the time we reached the flat. I introduced Sappho, showed him the bathroom, told him to strip off, threw in some stuff I'd got for the purpose – thick sweaters, cord trousers – the sort of stuff do-gooders wear – and went off to heat some tomato soup, and while he was sitting on the sofa scoffing it I slipped up behind him and put him out of his misery.

Cruel? I don't think so. He's neither cold nor hungry now. Nobody wanted him, so nobody will miss him, and there's one less dosser to clutter up the place.

Who loses?

I'd seen lots of movies where the character who's on the road picks up casual work in towns he's passing through. Washing dishes. Cutting firewood. Sweeping. I couldn't believe that in a city the size of London it might be impossible for a guy to find that sort of work. I mean, the place is packed with restaurants, caffs and kebab houses, not counting all the pubs. During my two weeks in Wharfedale Road I must've tried two hundred of them, starting with those in the King's Cross area. I got nowhere. Nowhere at all. As the days passed I widened the area of my search, and by halfway through the second week I'd been as far north as St John's Wood and south into Lambeth. I'd tramped the narrow little streets of Soho and the boulevards of South Kensington from early morning (I thought potential employers might be impressed by my willingness to be out and about early) till late at night. I'd offered my services in sleazy greasy caffs and posh hotels and everything in between till my feet felt bruised and I could hardly drag myself out of bed in a morning. I walked everywhere to save money. I lived on cheese rolls and tea, but I was down to nine quid and some change when rat-face came for his rent.

It was Friday night. Eight o'clock. I'd just got in. The room was freezing cold and I was treating myself to a quick burst of the cash-gobbling electric fire before bed when there was this knock on the door. I opened up and it was him. He said two words, 'Evening,' and 'Rent.'

I looked at him. 'It's only Friday,' I said. 'I'm paid on till Monday.'

He shook his head. 'Friday's rent day, sunshine.'

'But I moved in on a Monday,' I protested. 'And paid two weeks. That makes the room mine till Sunday night.'

He moved so quickly I hadn't time to step back. One second there was a yard of space between us, and the next he had a bunch of my shirt in his fist and his face was an inch from mine. 'Listen sunshine,' he hissed. 'The room's mine. I make the rules around here and the rent's due. If you've got it, pay up. If you haven't I'll give you five minutes to pack your stuff and get out.' He shoved me and followed me in, leaving the door open.

I tried to reason with him – told him I was waiting a decision by the DSS. He laughed. 'You're waiting, son,' he snarled. 'I'm not.' I said I was looking for work and pointed out that I'd been quiet and kept the room tidy. I didn't know what I was saying, really, I was that desperate, but it was no good. He told me to pack my bag and stood there with his arms folded while I did it.

When I'd finished I brushed past him on my way to the door and said, 'I'll have you for this. Sooner or later, one way or another I'll have you.' His laughter rang in my ears as I went down the stairs.

And that's how I came to join them – the homeless kids I'd seen everywhere on my travels. The kids I'd given change to a week ago when I'd thought things were bound to work out. I was one of them now – poised at the top of that downward spiral.

Daily Routine Orders 6

Time for a brief discourse on the subject of killing. Killing humans. Murder, not to put too fine a point on it.

Oh yes, that's what they'd call it. If they ever found out about it, which they won't. Murder. The deliberate killing by a human being of another human being. But you see, I was trained to kill. As a soldier, it was my chief function to kill, waste, do in – whatever you want to call it – those among my fellow humans whose activities happened to displease the powers that be in my country. And this is where the confusion arises. This is where distinctions get a bit blurred. The killing by a soldier of the enemies of his country is not murder. They don't jail you for it. In fact, if you do it really well they give you a medal. So why, if I'm disposing of these druggy dossers whose activities are dragging the country down, am I a murderer? It's all nonsense. I'm not a murderer at all – I'm a soldier out of uniform, killing for his country. Trouble is, is that because the country doesn't approve, the whole thing becomes a hole-and-corner affair. You've got to hide what you're doing, and that brings us to the hard part, which is DISPOSING OF THE BODY.

You see, soldiers – soldiers in uniform – don't have this problem. They don't have to conceal the bodies of their victims. Quite the reverse in fact. They lay 'em out in rows, count 'em, take snapshots of 'em, like shooting parties used to do with pheasant. Only difference is they don't eat 'em. They shove 'em in a big hole and bury 'em and that's that. No problem.

21

Everyone knows they're there, nobody cares. But if you're out of uniform, like me – if you're what they call a murderer – you've got to get rid of the body, and that's a real worry because, believe it or not, it's far and away the hardest bit of the whole job.

Killing's easy. Dead easy. Especially if you've been trained to it, though of course anyone can do it if they put their mind to it, but more murderers have come unstuck because they made a mess of disposing of the body than through any other cause. It's a fact.

Everything's been tried. Acid baths. Dismemberment. Cement boots and a deep river. Everything. And more often than not it's no use – the body (or parts of it) turns up sooner or later and the killer is caught.

I won't be. No. Because unlike most so-called murderers, I've planned in advance. My flat's on the ground floor, and there's a handy little space – quite a big space, actually – under the floorboards. It's beautifully ventilated – stick your hand down there and you feel the draught – so it'll stay cool, even on the warmest day. That's important. I won't go into why because it's not a pleasant subject – let's just say bodies in a warm place have a way of betraying their presence after a day or two. So – I've got this place – I like to think of it as my built-in refrigerator – and that's where our little friend of last night now lies. As I have said, he doesn't feel the cold, nor is he cluttering up anyone's doorway. The whole thing's so much tidier, don't you think?

I found a doorway. A good deep one, so deep that light from street-lamps and shopfronts didn't reach the door itself and you could sit with your back against it and not be seen by passers-by.

It was nine o'clock, and cold. I sat on my bed-roll with my backpack between my feet, watching the bright narrow rectangle of movement and colour at the end of my little tunnel. People passed continuously but nobody glanced my way. Nobody knew I was there. Across the street I could see subway railings with a news-vendor's pitch, a road junction and part of King's Cross Station. I sat thinking about my rat-faced former landlord who couldn't spell negotiation – about how one day I'd catch him unawares in a dark alleyway, and about the inventive and wondrous things I'd do to him there. I was angry and a bit shaken, I suppose, but I wasn't particularly unhappy. Not then. My anonymity was a comfort – at least I wasn't going to be seen by people who knew me. Also, I was one among many. My plight could have no curiosity value for anybody who might spot me. And there was no further need to fret about next week's rent. I felt – free, I suppose. This was before I became acquainted with some of the setbacks, like hunger pangs and real cold and the problem of what to do when you have to go to the lavatory and guard your bedroom at the same time. It was this last one which got to me first and lost me my doorway and more besides.

As I've said, I found my lovely doorway around nine o'clock, and for a time it was okay sitting there watching the world go by. In fact it was quite pleasant in a way. But by eleven my feet and legs were cold, I was tired, my bed-roll was giving me a numb bum and I was dying for a pee. I saw no problem, though. The station was just across the way. There'd be toilets in there somewhere. All I had to do was stroll across. The numbness would go and the walk would warm me up. 'Course I'd have to take my stuff. If I left it back here in the dark it might be all right, but you can't take that sort of chance when your bed-roll and backpack are all you have in the world. So.

Quarter past eleven I got up and toted my stuff across to the station. The Gents turned out to be half-way down platform one, but there was no barrier so I motored on down, passing some down-and-outs sitting on benches. The place was underground. I trotted down the steps, beginning to relax like you do when you know relief is imminent, and hit snag one. At the foot of the stairs was a turnstile. Ten pence. I dropped my roll and fished in my pockets. A fifty, two twenties and some copper. No ten. There was a glass box – a sort of office, so there must be an attendant. I called out, 'Excuse me?' My predicament was becoming acute. There was no answer. Nothing stirred. I glanced all round, chucked my roll over the stile and followed it.

The relief was terrific. Half-way through, the door of a cubicle opened and out popped a runty little guy of about fifty with a peaked cap and a fag hanging out of his gob. ''Ere,' he croaked. ''Ave you paid?'

'N-no,' I stammered. He'd made me splash my trainers. 'I haven't got –'

'I don't give a toss what you haven't got, son.'

He was really hoarse – a sixty-a-day man. I could probably push him over with one hand. I'd been about to ask him to change twenty pence, but his attitude upset me. I decided I'd vault the stile and save myself ten p. 'I've no dosh,' I told him, zipping up.

He stood in front of the turnstile. 'You don't leave till you've paid.' His fag wagged up and down as he spoke, sifting ash down his front. I looked at him. 'Get out the way, old man.'

He shook his head. More ash. I moved towards him, swinging my roll. He dodged and swung an inept punch at my head. I ducked, shoved him aside and vaulted the stile.

I felt terrific – streetwise and tough – but I daren't linger in the station. I pictured him in his glass box, phoning the railway police. I hurried back up the platform and out to the street.

When I got back to my doorway somebody was there. I didn't see him till I kicked his foot. He leapt up. A six-footer, as wide as the door. 'What's yer problem, wack?'

'I – I was here first.' God, what a stupid thing to say. He poked me in the chest. 'Sod off, kiddo, before I drop yer.'

'But I've been here two hours,' I protested. 'I just went in the station for a –'

'Sod off – now!'

I knew I'd have to go, too. This was no chain-smoking runt you could knock down with a feather. This guy was what I'd been kidding myself I'd become – a streetwise tough. I turned away with a lump in my throat. I felt like I'd spend the rest of my life being pushed around. 'It's not fair,' I choked.

What a wally I was. Fair! If I'd gone straight away he might not have spotted the watch on my wrist, but he did. He grabbed my sleeve. 'Nice watch. Gizzit.'

'No!' The watch was my last treasure – a present from Mum before Vince came on the scene. I tried to pull away but he tightened his grip. 'Gizzit, if you don't want your face smashed in.'

I thought about calling for help. There were plenty of people passing, but I guess I knew it would do no good. Who's going to risk a fist or a knife to help a dosser? I took off the watch and handed it over. It was a struggle not to burst into tears. He grinned. 'Ta, wack. Very nice of yer. Now piss off.'

I went.

It's like parachuting. Get the first jump over and it becomes routine, but you mustn't get complacent. Check your equipment every time. Run through procedures. Know what's what. Don't fall into any traps.

There's a trap serial killers fall into, namely, the trap of pattern. There's something the same about each of their killings, and this tells the law that it's the same person doing them. It also helps the police by saying something about the killer. For example, if all his victims are Mexican they know they're probably looking for a bloke who hates Mexicans. If all the bodies are found in underground stations, they're after someone who hangs around underground stations. It's a trap, see? A trap of the killer's own making, because it narrows the field.

I've got to be particularly careful about this. I can't help making a pattern, because all of my clients are dossers. Bound to be. Of course, they're not going to find bodies, in underground stations or anywhere else. I'm not that daft. But there is this unavoidable pattern, so what I have to do is create as much variety as possible without straying beyond the borders of my appointed task.

Last night's piece of business differed from its predecessor in several respects. For one thing, my client was a female. I didn't select her because I like women, or because I hate them. I can take them or leave them, as a matter of fact. I chose her because the last one was a male, that's all. And I didn't pick her up by Camden tube, because that's another pattern. I rode down to Piccadilly Circus and strolled round Soho, and I spotted her coming out of the Regent Palace. Manky, she was – you could see the grime on her neck from across the road – and there she was, stepping out of the hotel like a bleeding duchess or something. She'd sneaked in to use the toilet of course, but how she'd got past security I don't know. Anyway, I let her get a little way down the road before tapping her on the shoulder.

'Excuse me.' She spun round.

'Y-yes?'

'Hotel Security,' I snapped. 'Regent Palace.' Well, I looked the part in my suit and trenchcoat. 'You were in the hotel just now, weren't you?'

She nodded. There was a look in her eyes like a hunted animal. 'Yes. I went to the toilet. Why?'

'There's been a series of thefts. I'm afraid I must ask you to return with me to the hotel.'

'Thefts?' She looked desperate. 'I don't know anything about thefts. I told you – I needed the toilet. I was only there for a minute.' Poor cow. Looking as she did, she must have stuck out like a sore thumb in there. She wouldn't have lasted long enough to commit theft.

'I'm sorry,' I said. 'But you must come with me and answer some questions. It won't take long.'

'Oh, God!' She bit her lip. 'Look – I'm in enough trouble as it is. I'm homeless, I have no job and no money. I've nothing on me. Can't you just search me or something and let me go?'

She was close to tears, as they say in the bodice-rippers. I judged it was time to pull my master stroke. I eyed her up and down, speculatively. 'Hmm. Wouldn't mind searching you, at that,' I purred. 'Homeless, you say?'

She nodded. I could see the dawn of hope in her eyes.

'Nasty night too. How'd you fancy spending it in a cosy flat?' I was brilliant. 'Nice warm bed?'

'What d'you mean?' She knew what I meant. I smiled and she said, 'You mean you want me to –?'

I shrugged. 'It was just a thought, petal. You get off the hook as a suspect and I get –' I smiled again.

She hesitated, but it didn't take her long to see how poor her alternatives were. She probably believed I'd fit her up on a theft charge if she opted to come the puritan. She nodded, looking down, and mumbled 'Okay.'

The rest was simple. Taxi back to my place. Sappho. Dry clothing. Tomato soup. Eternal oblivion.

They look so sweet, the two of them side by side, that I keep going down for another look. I must be getting soft.

I trudged along Pentonville Road, peering into doorways and the entrances to office blocks. My left wrist felt naked without the watch and I added the scouser to my hit list. Rat-face and the scouser. I was going to turn into a serial killer if I went on at this rate.

After a bit I came to a doorway which was both deep and unoccupied. I dodged into it and stood there, wondering whether I dare doss down. What if this was somebody's bedroom too? Somebody big, like the scouser? Suppose he showed up and took a fancy to my pack, my bed-roll, and demanded them? Or he might just knife me and take them. On the other hand it was now pretty late, though of course I didn't know what time exactly. Surely, I told myself, if somebody dossed here regularly he'd be here by now? Anyway, I was dead tired. I had to get my head down somewhere, and wherever I went there was going to be this same doubt. So.

I'd just wriggled into my sleeping-bag and dropped my head on my pack when he arrived. I heard these footsteps and thought, keep going. Go past. Please go past, but he didn't. The footsteps stopped and I knew he was looking down at me. I opened my eyes. He was just a shadow framed in the doorway. 'This your place?' I croaked. Stupid question. He was going to say yes even if it wasn't, right? What I should have said was piss off. I wondered how big he was.

'No, you're right, mate.' He sounded laid back, amiable. 'Just shove up a bit so I can spread my roll.' I obliged and he settled himself beside me, so close we were almost touching. It felt good to be with someone. Now, if anybody else turned up it wouldn't matter. There were two of us. I felt I ought to say something so I said, 'Been doing this long?' hoping he wouldn't be offended.

'Six, seven months,' he said. 'You?'

'First night.'

He chuckled. 'I can tell. Where you from?'

'Up north.'

'Brum, me.'

'I can tell.' It was a risk, this crack about his accent, but he only chuckled again. 'Name's Ginger,' he said, and waited.

I didn't want to give my name. Not to anybody. Clean break, right? Fresh start. And anyway, he hadn't told me his. Ginger's only a nickname.

'Link,' I said. I'd seen this signpost earlier. Thameslink. It's a railway.

'Oh, aye?' he said, meaning I don't believe you but it's not heavy. 'Got a fag on you, Link?'

'Don't smoke.' For once I wished I did.

He laughed again. 'You will.'

'How d'you mean?'

'Been hungry, have you? I mean, really hungry?'

'No.'

'No. Well, when you are, smoking helps. Dulls the pain a bit.'

'Ah. You hungry now, Ginger?'

'Bit. Why – you got grub?'

'Got a Snicker in my pack. D'you want it?'

'Don't you?'

'No. Not hungry.' This wasn't completely true, but I

31

thought perhaps I'd found a friend and I wanted to hang on to him. I opened my pack and groped about till I found the bar. 'Here.'

'Ta, mate. Sure you don't want it?'

'No.'

'Half?'

'No – you eat it.' I buckled my pack and lay with my eyes closed, listening to him eat. He was pretty hungry at that. You could tell. When he'd finished he said, ''S better. G'night, Link.'

'Night, Ginger.'

And that's how I met Ginger.

I must have slept, because the next thing I knew somebody was nudging me none too gently in the back, saying 'Come on, sunshine – let's have you.' I opened my eyes and instantly screwed them shut as torchlight lanced into them. My first thought was that Ginger had changed his mind and wanted me out of his bedroom, but then my mind cleared and I knew it was the police. I sat up. It was still dark, and bitterly cold as I began to peel off my sleeping-bag.

There were two officers – a man and a woman. Once they'd got us awake they stood back and watched while we rolled our bags and strapped them to our packs. 'Don't forget that,' grunted the guy, shining his torch on the screwed-up wrapper from my Snicker. Ginger picked it up and shoved it in his pocket. I thought they were going to arrest us or something, but as soon as we were packed and on our feet they moved off, shining their torches into doorways as they went.

'What time is it?' I asked as we stood, dazed with cold and sleep in the orange light of a street-lamp.

Ginger shook his head. 'Dunno. About six, probably.'

'Why'd they do that? Get us up, I mean.'

'Why?' He grimaced. 'We were in somebody's doorway. Wouldn't do for the owner or tenant or whatever to find us here when he came to open up, would it?'

I couldn't think of any answer to that, so I said, 'What now?'

He looked at me. 'You got any money?'

I nodded. 'Nine quid and some change.'

'Fancy a coffee – bite to eat?'

'Not half.' I was starving. 'You?'

He smiled. 'You don't have to feed me, y'know, just 'cause we shared a doorway. Folks like us, we've got to look after number one. And don't tell anybody else you've got nine quid or you won't have it long.'

We went to an all-night kebab house he knew about. It was warm and glaringly bright inside and smelled so good I practically drooled. The clock on the wall said 06.20. We were the only customers.

We bolted doner and slurped coffee and talked. Ginger asked me what I planned to do. I told him I was looking for work while waiting for the DSS to come to a decision about my case. When I told him what I'd told them about my circumstances he shook his head. 'Waste of time, mate. Foregone conclusion. They'll say you made yourself homeless 'cause you left your mum's place voluntarily.'

'You mean I'll get no benefit – nothing?'

'Not a sausage, mate, you can take it from me. I've seen it too many times.'

'But – if I don't find work – if it takes a while – how'm I supposed to live?'

He laughed. 'Any way you can, Link old son. Nobody cares, see? Nobody gives a toss. That's the first thing you've gotta learn.' He smiled. 'Why d'you think so many kids beg the punters for change? 'Cause they like it?'

I shook my head. 'Is that what you do – beg?'

'Yep. All day, every day. And sometimes I don't make the price of a sandwich.'

'Do – do most people refuse, then?'

'Oh, aye.' He smiled again. 'Do you know what a solcredulist is?'

'No.'

'A solcredulist is someone who believes what he reads in the *Sun*. And do you know what the *Sun* says – the *Sun* and three or four other tabloids?'

I shook my head.

'Well, I'll tell you. They say us kids aren't homeless at all. They say we trick the punters out of their change all day and go home to our mums at night with forty, fifty quid in our pockets, and it all goes on drink and drugs.'

'They don't?'

'They bloody do, you know. And the solcredulists believe 'em, and all. That's why they refuse.'

'But it's a lie,' I cried. 'There ought to be a law against it.'

'True.' He laughed. 'There won't be, though. It's what they call the freedom of the press.'

I looked at him. 'So when my dosh runs out, I'll be begging too, huh?'

'I wouldn't wait till it runs out, mate. Like I said, some days you'll make sod-all. I'd start today if I was you.'

We lingered in the warmth till breakfast-time customers began drifting in and the proprietor started giving us dirty looks.

'Come on,' said Ginger. 'We don't want to outstay our welcome or he'll bar us.' He got up and shouldered his pack. 'There's a nice washroom through the back here. I'll show you.'

We used the washroom and left the kebab house just as it was starting to get light. I tagged along with Ginger through the early rush, hoping he'd let me stick with him today. I'd a feeling he knew a lot of stuff I'd need to learn if I was to survive in this great, cold jungle.

It was a raw morning with a sneaky wind which came out of side streets and went right through you. I thought Ginger was looking for a good spot to sit – somewhere out of the wind with plenty of passers-by, but we just kept walking. We were going south and I thought, I wish England wasn't an island, then we could just keep going till we came to Spain or North Africa – somewhere warm and sunny. After a while I said, 'Where we off?' and he said, 'Don't matter. This weather, gotta keep moving.'

It was daylight now and there were plenty of people about. I started noticing how a lot of them would alter course so they wouldn't pass too close to us. Now and then Ginger would change course too and intercept some guy. 'Got any spare change, mate?' he'd ask, and nearly always the guy would go on by without giving anything.

For something to do, I began studying their various responses. Some would simply walk on glassy-eyed and expressionless, as though Ginger wasn't there. Some assumed angry expressions, compressing their lips and sweeping by as though grossly insulted. There were head-shakers, pocket-patters and shruggers, who demonstrated through mime the absence of coins in their pockets; and there were those who'd mutter unintelligibly, so that you couldn't tell whether they'd said sorry no change or bugger off. Once Ginger accosted a stiff, military-looking guy who stopped, looked him up and down as if he was something the cat sicked up and said 'Change? I'd change you my lad, if I had you in khaki for six weeks.' There were lots of solcredulists about.

Now and then though, somebody would fork out a few coppers. The givers came in two types – the disdainful and the apologetic. The disdainful type would look down his nose at you, fish in his pocket, drop some coppers in your hand saying 'There,' and move on with his head in the air. The apologetic type would look embarrassed and fumble out a fistful of coins, saying something like, 'I'm sorry – this is all I have,' or 'Sorry, but you see I gave earlier – young man in a doorway.' He'd dump the dosh in Ginger's hand without looking to see how much there was and smile apologetically as he moved off. One such giver glanced at me with a worried expression, as though wondering whether he should have given to me, too.

We covered some miles that morning, trudging half frozen down Tottenham Court Road and on to Shaftesbury Avenue. We crossed Piccadilly Circus and set off along Piccadilly till Ginger stopped and nodded at some fancy iron gates and said, 'Here we are, mate.'

'Looks like a church,' I said.

He chuckled. 'It is. St James's. We can take the weight off our feet, get out of this wind.'

'Will they let us?'

'Yeah. You can get your head down in a pew if you want, in the daytime. Locked at night, though.'

We went in. It was lovely inside – white and gold and clean looking, with vases of flowers and polished woodwork. The only person in there was a battered wino who sat hunched in a pew near the back, muttering to himself. He took no notice of us as we walked down the aisle, slipped into a pew and shrugged off our packs. It was a relief to sit down, and great to be out of the icy wind. I was amazed we'd been able to just walk in like that. I felt like I was there under false pretences and wondered if I should pray or something, but Ginger winked and grinned and started counting the change he'd collected.

'One pound seventy-four pence,' he announced. 'And a peso. We can have cheese rolls for lunch, Link old son. They do an outstanding cheese roll here.'

'Here?' I thought he was putting me on.

'Oh, yes. There's a caff tagged on the side.'

'Never.'

'There is. Go look if you don't believe me.'

I shook my head. 'You're the expert. I believe you, only that's your dosh, not mine. I didn't do a thing.'

He looked at me. 'Who paid for breakfast?'

'Well I did, but –'

'No buts. I pay, you fetch.' He smiled. 'You look more respectable than me. They'll take you for a tourist.'

There was a café, and they did an outstanding cheese roll. We ate in church, which felt disrespectful, but I eased my conscience by telling myself that Jesus ate in people's houses so he wouldn't mind if someone ate in His. I was happy, I guess, right then. I had a friend, a full belly and a roof over my head. Who could ask for more?

It has happened again. I was on my way to inspect theatreland when two dossers approached me. One – the scruffier of the two – asked me for change. I responded in my usual way, and as I passed on I distinctly heard them laughing. I hope for their sakes that they manage to retain that sense of humour because they'll need it quite soon. I never forget a face, and our next meeting will prove far more amusing for me than for them.

By golly it will.

We sat in St James's till two o'clock. It wasn't warm, but we were out of the wind. Then Ginger said, 'I'm gonna try round Trafalgar Square for a bit. Coming?'

I nodded. 'If it's okay with you. It's time I had a go at getting some dosh by myself, but I'll feel better if you're somewhere around.'

He nodded. 'Fair enough. Tell you what – you try outside the National Gallery. It's not exactly the height of the tourist season but there are always people about, and you can see into the square from the steps.'

We walked back along Piccadilly, down the Haymarket and along Pall Mall. The Gallery wasn't fantastically busy but there was a steady trickle of people going in and out. Some were sitting on the steps in spite of the cold. Ginger left me there. I watched him merge with the crowd, then turned my attention to the business of the day.

It was hard at first. Really hard. I stood, watching people pass, trying to spot a likely punter. God knows what I was looking for – a kind face, I suppose, or at least someone who didn't look as though he'd swear or punch me in the mouth. It was futile, of course. You can't read people's characters in their faces. You never know what a punter's reaction is going to be, but I didn't know that then. Finally, I steeled myself and asked a guy at random. He growled, 'Not a chance,' and bounded up the steps, taking them two at a time. I wasted the next five minutes feeling hurt. Rejected.

I asked myself how it was possible for a person to be sensitive to the beauty of fine art, and at the same time insensitive to the feelings of a fellow creature. I took it personally, which is fatal. After a while I realized this and began choosing guys and women at random, expecting nothing, telling them to have a nice day whether they gave or refused. I blunted the point of my own sensitivity in the flinty soil of their indifference till I too became indifferent, and after that it was easier.

I worked till the Gallery closed, standing sometimes, sometimes sitting on the steps. My feet became numb and I was half frozen but I stuck at it, and when the place closed at dusk and the punters drifted away I counted up and found I'd collected just under four pounds. I stumped across to the Square and found Ginger slumped on a bench. He looked up as I approached.

'How'd it go?'

I shrugged. 'Three pounds eighty-one. You?'

'Two forty-four and I'm frozen to the bone. Let's eat.'

We got pizza slices and coke. When Ginger wasn't looking I bought twenty fags and a cheapo lighter and gave them to him. He said, 'You're barmy, kiddo. You don't even smoke.' I was just glad of his company, but I didn't say so.

In the evening the wind strengthened and sleet began to fall, except that it didn't fall – it rode the wind in horizontal lines, flaying foreheads and cheeks. I wished we were back in St James's but Ginger said it'd be locked now. We ended up in the doorway of a shop called Chinacraft on the Strand, huddled in our bags, waiting for the Vaudeville Theatre to close. 'Over there,' said Ginger through chattering teeth, 'are some alcoves, right? Deep ones. Good kip, only you've got to be here early.'

He lit a cigarette, took a deep drag and passed it to me. I hesitated and he chuckled, exhaling smoke. 'Go on – might as well. You'll not see sixty anyway, dossing in doorways.'

I took a drag and started choking, and he laughed. 'See what I mean?' he said. 'You're half-way there already.'

If you think sleeping rough's just a matter of finding a dry spot where the fuzz won't move you on and getting your head down, you're wrong. Not your fault of course – if you've never tried it you've no way of knowing what it's like, so what I thought I'd do was sort of talk you through a typical night. That night in the Vaudeville alcove won't do, because there were two of us and it's worse if you're by yourself.

So you pick your spot. Wherever it is (unless you're in a squat or a derelict house or something) it's going to have a floor of stone, tile, concrete or brick. In other words it's going to be hard and cold. It might be a bit cramped, too – shop doorways often are. And remember, if it's winter you're going to be half frozen before you even start. Anyway you've got your place, and if you're lucky enough to have a sleeping-bag you unroll it and get in.

Settled for the night? Well maybe, maybe not. Remember my first night? The Scouser? 'Course you do. He kicked me out of my bedroom and pinched my watch. Well, that sort of thing can happen any night, and there are worse things. You could be peed on by a drunk or a dog. Happens all the time – one man's bedroom is another man's lavatory. You might be spotted by a gang of lager louts on the look-out for someone to maim. That happens all the time too, and if they get carried away you can end up dead. There are the guys who like young boys, who think because you're a dosser you'll do anything for dosh, and there's the psycho who'll knife you for your pack.

So, you lie listening. You bet you do. Footsteps. Voices. Breathing, even. Doesn't help you sleep.

Then there's your bruises. What bruises? Try lying on a stone floor for half an hour. Just half an hour. You can choose any position you fancy, and you can change position as often as you like. You won't find it comfy, I can tell you. You won't sleep unless you're dead drunk or zonked on downers. And if you are, and do, you're going to wake up with bruises on hips, shoulders, elbows, ankles and knees – especially if you're a bit thin from not eating properly. And if you do that six hours a night for six nights you'll feel like you fell out of a train. Try sleeping on concrete then.

And don't forget the cold. If you've ever tried dropping off to sleep with cold feet, even in bed, you'll know it's impossible. You've got to warm up those feet, or lie awake. And in January, in a doorway, in wet trainers, it can be quite a struggle. And if you manage it, chances are you'll need to get up for a pee, and then it starts all over again.

And those are only some of the hassles. I haven't mentioned stomach cramps from hunger, headaches from the flu, toothache, fleas and lice. I haven't talked about homesickness, depression or despair. I haven't gone into how it feels to want a girl-friend when your circumstances make it virtually impossible for you to get one – how it feels to know you're a social outcast in fact, a non-person to whom every ordinary everyday activity is closed.

So. You lie on your bruises, listening. Trying to warm your feet. You curl up on your side and your hip hurts, so you stretch out on your back so your feet stay cold and the concrete hurts your heels. You force yourself to lie still for a bit, thinking that'll help you drop off, but it doesn't. Your pack feels like a rock under your head and your nose is cold. You wonder what time it is. Can you stop listening now, or could someone still come? Distant chimes. You strain your ears, counting. One o'clock? It can't be only one o'clock, surely? I've been here hours. Did I miss a chime?

What's that? Sounds like breathing. Heavy breathing, as in maniac. Lie still. Quiet. Maybe he won't see you. Listen. Is he still there? Silence now. Creeping up, perhaps. No. Relax. Jeez, my feet are cold.

A thought out of nowhere – my old room at home. My little bed. What I wouldn't give for – no, mustn't. Mustn't think about that. No sleep that way. Somebody could be asleep in that room right now. Warm and dry. Safe. Lucky sod.

Food. God, don't start on about food! (Remember that time in Whitby – fish and chip caff? Long, sizzling haddock, heap of chips like a mountain. So many, you had to leave some. Wish I had them now.)

Mum. Wonder what Mum's doing? Wonder if she wonders where I am? How would she feel if she knew? I miss you, Mum. Do you miss me? Does anybody?

Chimes again. Quarter past. Quarter past one? I don't believe it.

DSS. Are they considering my claim? (Not now they're not – they're sleeping. Snug as a bug in a rug.) Do they know what it feels like, kipping in a doorway? No.

And so it goes on, hour after hour. Now and then you doze a bit, but only a bit. You're so cold, so frightened and it hurts so much that you end up praying for morning even though you're dog-tired – even though tomorrow is certain to be every bit as grim as yesterday.

And the worst part is knowing you haven't deserved any of it.

I walked all the way back to the DSS next morning and Ginger was right. I was seen by this guy who told me they'd decided I'd made myself homeless so I wasn't eligible for benefit. I hadn't intended spilling my guts but I did then. I was dirty, cold and hungry and my feet were killing me. I was so tired I could hardly string a coherent sentence together. I'd had enough, so I told him everything – Vince and Mum, Vince and Carole, Vince and me. I thought he'd see – thought he'd understand why I could never go back into that situation, but I might as well have been talking to one of the stone lions in Trafalgar Square. He just sat there looking at me through his blue-tinted specs, and when I'd finished he repeated word for word and without facial expression what he'd said to me before.

I'd arranged to meet Ginger by Cleopatra's Needle. The weather was vile and I hadn't the heart for another long walk so I got the tube at Euston and rode down to the Embankment. I was early and he wasn't there, so I spent a miserable couple of hours begging along the river, getting colder and wetter and nothing else. In the end I gave up and went and sat under a bridge in an icy draught. Ginger had given me two fags, so I cadged a light and smoked them both, lighting the second off the first. I was starving and the smoke made me nauseous, but it was comforting, too, in a way I couldn't be bothered thinking about. When the fags were gone I counted my dosh and found I was down to four quid – four pounds sixteen pence if you want it exact. I was desperate for something to eat and also needed a lavatory, so I set off hoping to find a hot-dog stand or something. I found a public toilet easily enough and washing my hands and face made me feel a bit better, but I didn't find any food.

I trailed back to the Needle and this time Ginger was there, sitting on his pack with a dustbin bag draped over his head and shoulders. 'Like the new outfit,' I said.

'Fetching, isn't it?' He got up and gave me a twirl. 'Burlington Arcade. Four hundred quid. How'd you get on?'

I told him and he shrugged. 'That's it, then. You'll have to give backword on Buckingham Palace, go for something more compact, like a cardboard box.'

He was starving too, so we left the river and trogged north for pizza. It was dusk already. We ate in a doorway and he said, 'How'd you like a proper kip tonight, Link old son – roof over your head, the works?'

I looked at him. 'Sally Army or something?'

'Naw!' He shook his head. 'Bad news, them places. Full of raving head-cases. Spent a night in one once – scared me to death. No – I was thinking of Captain Hook.'

'Who?'

'Captain Hook.'

I looked at him. 'Go on then – I'll fall for it. Who's Captain Hook?'

He shook his head, grinning. 'It's not a put-on, mate. He's a real guy. Get us a quick coffee and I'll tell you all about him.'

Three is a significant number. It crops up in all sorts of places. Three cheers. The Three Musketeers. If I had three wishes. Three blind mice. The Blessed Trinity. The three armed services. The three little pigs. A significant number.

I have three recruits now. When I had one I was a murderer, two, a double murderer, and now that I've got three I suppose I'm a mass-murderer – what the Yanks call a serial killer. If they caught me now, which they won't, they'd probably make a film about me.

Naturally, I've arranged them the Army way – tallest on the left, shortest on the right and they look quite smart – especially now that I've cut their hair. I'll have to try to get them some boots, or at least proper shoes – something which will take a shine. At the moment they're all wearing those manky trainer things.

Last night's bit of business – signing up recruit number three – gave me particular pleasure. You'll know why presently, but let me start at the beginning. It was about 20.00 hours and I'd just begun my nightly patrol. It was an unpleasant evening – wind and sleet – exactly the sort of evening one needs in my line of work. I'd walked into Gloucester Avenue and down the steps on to the towpath of the Grand Union Canal, intending to stroll along by Camden Lock to see what I could see when I spotted him. He was a miserable looking creature – thin and round-shouldered with rat-tails of greasy hair halfway down his back. He had some pieces of cardboard which he was arranging on the ground under the stairs I'd just descended. It was fairly dry there and it was obvious he was setting up a billet for the night. I had on my do-gooder's rig and I approached him, looking concerned. 'Surely,' I said, 'you don't intend spending a night like this in a place like that?'

He was suspicious. Oh, yes. He looked at me and I knew straightaway he wasn't new to the game. 'You got a better idea?' he growled.

I shrugged, putting on my best apologetic grin. 'No offence,' I said. 'It's just that it's so cold, and I wondered whether you'd tried your luck at the Plender Street hostel.'

'There's no hostel on Plender Street,' he said. 'And besides, hostels are always full up by this time.' He gazed at me. 'What's it to you, anyway? What's your game, Grandad?'

'No game.' I smiled my woolly-headed smile. 'There is a hostel on Plender Street. It's new, so not many people know about it yet. That's why it's not full.'

'How do you know so much?'

'I'm the Warden,' I lied. 'I run the place.'

'Why you not there, then?'

Oh, he was canny, this one. I'd need all my talent.

'I have to call home,' I said. 'Feed Sappho. We don't live in, you see.'

'Sappho?'

'My cat.'

He snorted. 'Fugging cat sleeps warmer than me. Eats better too.' He studied me. 'So you run this hostel?'

'Right.'

'And it's not full?'

'Not when I left.'

'Gotta be a catch.' He looked at me sidelong. 'How much?'

47

I shook my head. 'Nothing. No catch. It's a free hostel. Breakfast, too.'

'So if I go along –?'

I grinned. 'If you go along you'll probably be fine. If you arrive with me it's a cert.'

'Where d'you live, then?'

'Not far. Mornington Place. Know it?'

He nodded. 'I know it. Okay – I'm in, only you better be on the level, Grandad, 'cause if you ain't I'll kick your tripes out.'

So he abandoned his cardboard and shouldered his pack and we walked, and as we walked we talked.

'Whereabouts you from?' I enquired. I didn't give a damn where he was from – I knew exactly where he was going.

'Leicester.'

'Leicester? No work there, eh?'

He shook his head. 'Six months I was, writing letters, going for interviews. No chance.'

'So you thought you'd try London?'

'Not straightaway. I tried the Army first.'

Well, you can be sure my ears pricked up at that. I was genuinely interested now. 'The Army?' I said. 'And what happened?'

He shrugged. 'Couldn't stand it. Thick sods bawling at you all day long. Telling you what to do. And the grub – Jesus! So I bought myself out.'

'Hmm – well. Not everybody's cup of tea, the Army. Full of Fascists, I shouldn't wonder.' I was absolutely seething of course, but I didn't give myself away. I was magnificent. Thick sods, indeed!

'Dunno about Fascists,' he said. 'I'm not into politics, but you must have to be desperate to stay in that mob.' He spat in the gutter. 'Better off on the streets.'

Right, my lad, I thought. You don't know it, but

you're about to join another army. It's a very small army, but it doesn't rely on volunteers and you can't buy yourself out. By golly you can't.

I told myself, watch this one. He's not green, but it turned out easier than I expected. Soft sod squatted down on my kitchen floor to fondle the ruddy animal and I let him have it with the Kit-E-Kat tin. Well – trained to kill, see. Know the exact spot to go for.

And d'you know something? That lad looks a hundred per cent better with a short back and sides. His mum would be proud of him.

So I fetched a coffee from the pizza bar and we shared it and Ginger told me about Captain Hook.

'Seems this guy, Probyn's his real name, buys six beat-up old narrowboats a few years back for a song, intending to do 'em up and hire 'em out for canal holidays, but when he finds out how much it'll cost to do 'em up he decides not to bother. He has a better idea. He's seen all the kids sleeping rough and he thinks, I know. Floating doss-houses, right? Dry kips, out of the wind, safe from crazies, no hassle from the fuzz – three quid a night. So he rips out all the fittings to maximize floor space or deck space or whatever, and works out he can cram sixty kids on each boat – all under cover. Six boats. That's three hundred and sixty kids at three quid. One thousand and eight quid a night. Of course it doesn't work that way in practice. He's hardly ever full, even in winter, because it's not easy to score three quid and anyway some kids can't stand being closed in, but he's doing okay out of it just the same.'

Ginger broke off for a gulp of coffee and I said, 'But surely there's regulations? Fire and that? Is it legal, what he's doing?'

Ginger shrugged. 'Fire, health and hygiene – he must be well out of line, but nobody's bothered. I mean, he's getting kids off the streets, see? Packing 'em away where the tourists can't see 'em, so the powers that be turn a blind eye.'

'And where is this? Where's he got these boats?'

'By Camden Lock. D'you fancy it? Out of the weather for once?'

I shrugged. 'Sounds okay, yeah, but I'm low on dosh. Three quid for a kip'll clean me out.'

'No worries.' He grinned. 'I met this guy today, owed me a tenner. He didn't have it but he gave me seven. We're laughing.'

'He must be working.'

'Sort of, yeah. Sells the paper. *The Big Issue*. Sells it at fifty p, gets to keep thirty. Lucky sod.' He looked at me. 'Are we on, then?'

I nodded and we set off into the wind with our heads down, sharing Ginger's bin bag. Two lost boys, off to the never-never land.

Have you ever seen that famous diagram of a slave ship – slaves crammed like sardines into every square centimetre of space? Well, that's what it was like on the boat me and Ginger ended up on.

We'd parted with our six quid on the tow path, where Probyn had his office in one of those yellow plastic watchman shelters. He didn't look like Captain Hook. He was sitting on a folding canvas chair wearing wellies, a waxed jacket, a muffler, a knitted cap and gloves with the fingers cut out. He had a smooth, pink complexion and pale eyes and looked about thirty-five. When he smiled, as he did when he grabbed our dosh, he showed very small, very even white teeth. He stuffed the notes into a bulging wallet which he returned to an inside pocket. I was wondering why some guy hadn't mugged him for this when I heard a low growl and saw a Rottweiler the size of a horse gazing out from between his feet. Probyn showed his teeth again. 'Don't even think about it, kid,' he purred. He must've been a mind reader or something. Then he pointed to the nearest of his boats, moored fore and aft to bollards on the bank. 'That one,' he said. 'Mind the gap.'

I've told you it looked like a slave ship. What I haven't said is that it stank like one, too. You went through a narrow door and it hit you – the stench of too many damp, unwashed bodies, too much lingering flatulence. There were three steps down and then you were falling over sleepers, looking for a space in the poor light from a paraffin lamp which dangled unlawfully from the deckhead. We found a sliver of unoccupied floorspace and bedded down, drawing grunts and curses from those we kicked and elbowed in doing so.

One thing, though – it was certainly warm, and you weren't straining your ears all the time listening for potential assailants. The boat rocked very gently on the water, and once you stopped noticing the smell the whole thing was quite pleasant. It's amazing how resilient wooden planks feel after lying night after night on stone. I dropped off almost at once; and dreamt I was sailing my yacht through blue, tropic waters of breathtaking clarity under a cloudless sky, while Vince hurried back and forth with long, cool drinks for me, and my rat-faced former landlord cooled me with a peacock fan. It was terrific while it lasted, but waking up was a drag.

Has it ever struck you how much money people waste buying crap? I never really noticed till that Saturday after our night on the boat, when me and Ginger walked round the market.

Camden Lock market's famous, apparently, but I'd never heard of it till that morning. It's right beside the canal – a big site crammed with shops and stalls flogging all sorts of fancy stuff. Hats. Jewellery. Tee-shirts. Mirrors. Candles. Candles, for Chrissake. You name it, they've got it. A lot of the stuff's ethnic – Indian and so on – and they burn joss sticks all the time so the whole place smells of incense. It's only there weekends, and it attracts thousands of people.

Anyway, me and Ginger walk round and he says, 'No shortage of dosh here, Link old son. Money to burn. Breaks my heart how they chuck it away. Look.' I look where he's pointing and see fat, rainbow-coloured candles at four pounds twenty apiece. 'Four pounds twenty,' he laments. 'They'll refuse you ten pence towards a cup of tea, then spend four twenty on a bleedin' candle. Makes you weep.'

I chuckle, 'Why'd we come here, then, if it upsets you so much?'

He winks. 'Facilities, old son. Come on.'

I followed him up some steps and along a walkway and there were some immaculate toilets. We used the lavatories and had a proper wash. Ginger even washed out a pair of Y-fronts he produced from his pack. People were in and out all the time but nobody paid us any attention. I must have used about sixteen paper towels drying myself but I felt a whole lot better afterwards.

We're sipping scalding tea in one of the market cafés when three kids come in. Ginger knows them and calls out and they come and sit with us. Two guys and a girl, all with packs and that grey, zombie look you get from living on the street. Ginger doesn't introduce me and they ignore me, talking thirteen to the dozen with their chapped hands wrapped round steaming mugs. Where you been? How's it going? D'you ever see old what's-his-face nowadays? I sit gazing into my tea, feeling – what? Jealousy? Maybe. Apprehension, certainly. These are Ginger's friends. They've shared experiences. Have acquaintances in common. They know what he knows. What if he ditches me – goes off with them? If I was alone again, could I stand it? Do I know enough to get by?

A name comes up. A jokey name. Doggy Bag. 'D'you ever see Doggy Bag now?' asks Ginger, and the girl shakes her head.

'No,' she says. 'He vanished. One day he's in his usual doorway, next day gone.'

'Found work, maybe,' one of the guys suggests.

'Or moved on,' says the other. This closes the subject and the chat moves on, leaving me wondering how a guy gets a name like that.

They get up eventually, shrugging on their packs. We do the same. None of us wants to leave. It's warm in the café, but the proprietor's giving us dirty looks and we have no more dosh for tea, so we go before he can chuck us out. Outside, they say so long to Ginger and one of them nods to me and they're gone, melting into the crowd. Ginger's still here, and because I'm glad I smile and say, 'The guy you asked about – why'd they call him Doggy Bag?'

Ginger grins. 'He used to hang around cafés, and when somebody left he'd slip over to their table quick and drop their scraps in a plastic bag before the waitress came to clear. He couldn't bring himself to ask for change so that's how he lived, and that's why we christened him Doggy Bag.'

We left the market and trudged along the towpath and I started thinking about Doggy Bag, and after a bit I had to keep my face turned away from Ginger because I was afraid he'd see I was struggling to keep from crying. I know it sounds daft. I mean, I never knew the guy. Never even met him, but what I started thinking was this. I started thinking about how once, years ago, there was this baby, and his mum and dad loved him like mums and dads do, and they gave him a name and dreamed about what he'd be when he grew up and what his life would be like and all like that, and how they never dreamed he'd be called Doggy Bag and live on scraps and be so unimportant that he'd vanish and no one would care.

I do believe the mountain has come to Mohammed. Remember the two dossers I told you about – the ones who laughed at me in the Haymarket? Well, I spotted 'em this morning at Camden Lock, talking to some other scruffs. I know it was them – I never forget a face – and what I'm hoping is, two things. One, that they've moved into the area, and two, that they split up sometimes. I mean, I'm good at what I do. Damn good, but even I wouldn't fancy trying to recruit 'em two at a time.

See, you've got to know your enemy if you're going to lick him, and I know my enemy. I've observed him, and what I've observed is this. A lot of these dossers get together in twos, threes and fours and stick together. They might separate in the daytime – one might have to go to the DSS or somewhere – but at night they huddle together for warmth or protection or whatever. And of course you'd have to be barmy to approach 'em then, and I'm not barmy. By golly I'm not. No. Loners is what you look for in my line of business. Singletons. So I'm going to watch my laughing boys, and when they separate we'll see who has the last laugh.

The last days of January were a swine. I nearly went back to Vince. I mean it. It snowed every day so the pavements were thick with slush, and nothing gets inside a pair of trainers like slush can. Ginger and I lurked in subways and doorways as much as we could but our feet were constantly wet and freezing just the same. Night after night, frost turned the slush to grey iron and crept into our damp bedding to stiffen footwear and make sleep impossible. And if you think it's bound to make the punters more generous with their change, seeing kids wet and shivering, forget it. It had the opposite effect. Everybody slogged grimly by and their hands never left their pockets unless they were wearing gloves. Nobody stopped. Maybe they thought they'd die if they stopped, like explorers at the South Pole.

We grew hungry. Really hungry. The cold seems to settle in your bones when there's nothing in your stomach. You can't shift it. We tried everything – stamping our feet, running on the spot, blowing into our hands, huddling together in the subway. It was no use. All we could do was keep moving through sleepless nights and days that merged into one another till we no longer knew what day it was or whether it was morning or evening. One time, Ginger borrowed a marker pen from an old newsvendor and printed a couple of placards which read, NON-ALCOHOLIC HOMELESS, PLEASE HELP. He said you had to put non-alcoholic because people seldom give to winos. We sat in a subway somewhere with our feet and legs in our sleeping-bags and the placards on the muddy tiles, but he might as well have put EVIL, SHIFTLESS BABY-KICKER, AFTER YOUR DOSH for all the good it did us.

We stood on raw feet for hours outside various hostels, but there were always hundreds of kids and we never got a bed. I started hallucinating. For hours at a stretch I thought I was back on Captain Hook's foetid hulk. In lucid moments I'd gladly have given my right arm to be there, but I knew the Captain wasn't interested in right arms. Once we'd been turned away from a hostel, we'd make our way to one of the stations – King's Cross or St Pancras, mostly – to wait for the Sally Army. The walk would keep us from hypothermia, and the Sally Army came round about midnight with soup or sandwiches. It was free grub so there was always a mob, but we usually scored a butty apiece or a mug of soup, and that's what kept us alive till February came, and the thaw.

Oh, by the way, if you're wondering why I wasn't attending job interviews all this time, I can enlighten you. My clothes were sodden rags. My fingernails were long black claws, I had matted hair down to my shoulders and I stank. I wanted work all right – would have killed for it – but I knew I hadn't a hope in hell of being taken on in that condition. *I* wouldn't have hired me.

February wasn't a heatwave, either, but it stayed above freezing most of the time and we kept our feet dry. Tapping got a bit easier too. Not easy, but easier. I imagined I was becoming streetwise but I should've known better. I should've realized it was being with Ginger that was making things easy for me, but I didn't. Not until this day I'm going to tell about. The day Ginger vanished.

It began like any other day. We woke in a doorway when it was still dark, packed our gear and went for some coffee. We were dossing near Camden Station and there was this all-night café called the Brazilia where we'd sit warming up till it got light and we could start tapping. Anyway, this particular morning Ginger said, 'I'm meeting some mates down Holborn way this morning so I'll see you later, okay?'

I shrugged. 'Sure.' I didn't know who these mates were or when he'd fixed it up, but it was obvious he didn't want me along and I wasn't going to argue. The quickest way to lose a mate is to make yourself a drag, so I pretended I didn't give a toss. I did, though. It hurt like hell. I walked him along to the station and said, 'Have a nice day.' He grinned and nodded and the stream of early travellers swept him away and I never saw him again.

I spent the day trailing up and down the High Street, tapping. It was cold and blustery, but dry. I kept thinking about Ginger, wondering what he was doing with his mates in Holborn, and why he hadn't wanted me along. Maybe he's a dealer, I thought. Smack and crack. Ecstasy. Or maybe he's got this rich bird – an heiress or something – and they're shacked up right now in her luxury penthouse pad, tearing up lobsters and swilling champagne. I wasn't seriously worried. Not then. He'd gone off before and come back, but I'd be glad when this day was over just the same.

There's a clock outside the station. I looked at it every time I passed. At five thirty I stopped walking up and down. Some of the shops were just closing so I sat down in a doorway from which I could watch the station. I'd no idea what time he'd return, of course – it might be hours yet – but my feet were killing me and I had to sit somewhere. I could see the clock, so I kept an eye on that, too. I'd never known time pass so slowly.

At some point I fell asleep, and I must've slept a long time, because when the cold woke me it was after eleven and the station had closed. I'd no way of knowing whether Ginger had returned or not. I looked in all the usual kips and he wasn't in any of them. I couldn't face the night alone so I went to Captain Hook and surrendered every penny I had for a place on a boat, but this time there was no sweet dream.

Laughing Boy One. That was the code name of the exercise. It was meticulously planned and beautifully executed, and now it's time for de-briefing. In a well-regulated army, every operation is followed by a thorough de-briefing. A sort of inquest, if you'll pardon the grisly joke. So.

First, my intelligence work. The success of a given operation always depends on sound intelligence, and mine was a model of soundness. By golly it was. What I did was, I learned their names. Sounds simple, doesn't it? Elementary, but in fact it was absolutely crucial. I couldn't possibly have done what I did without it.

What did you do? I hear you ask. Well, it was simple. The best tactics are often the simplest. I dogged their footsteps till they separated. You remember I said a target must be alone? Well today, one of my laughing boys – Ginger – took the tube from Camden. At first I thought they were both going, but they parted at the station. The other scruff – Link, he calls himself, though Stink would be nearer the mark – started begging along the High Street. I went away for a while – the target obviously wouldn't be back for an hour or two at least – and then I came back and hung around, looking in shop windows and buying the occasional cup of char. This Link feller was still at it up and down the street and I kept well out of his way – I didn't want him noticing me.

It turned out to be a long wait, and it could all have been for nothing because Link just wouldn't bugger off. It started to get dark and I kept expecting him to leave, but he didn't. Eventually he sat down in a doorway opposite the station and I thought, terrific. Thanks a lot, you idle, useless prat. It was obvious he was waiting for his mate. I nearly gave up, but it's a good job I didn't because the pillock fell asleep, and not long after that I spotted my target coming out of the station. It was time for the master-plan.

I'm wearing my woolly-headed do-gooder rig. I run across the road and grab him by the arm, looking anxious. 'Excuse me,' I gabble. 'Are you Ginger, by any chance?'

'Who's asking?' he says. He can see I'm in a state but he's cagey just the same. I shake my head.

'Never mind,' I tell him. 'You're Link's mate, aren't you?'

He frowns. 'What's all this about? Is something wrong?'

I nod, pulling at his sleeve. 'It's Link,' I gasp. 'An accident. He ran right out in front of me. I never had a chance.'

He gawps at me. 'He – you mean you knocked him down? Is he dead?' It's his turn to grab my sleeve. 'Have you killed my mate, you bastard?'

'No, no.' I shake my head, pulling at him. 'Not dead. Not when I left. Badly hurt, though. Asking for you.'

'Where? Where is he? Is he in hospital or what?'

'No, my place. He's at my place. It happened right outside.'

'He's badly hurt and you've got him at your place?' He stares at me, wild-eyed. 'Why didn't you call an ambulance, you stupid git? He could be dying, for all you know. You better take me to him.'

I was magnificent though I say it myself. Here was a hard, streetwise kid, cagey as they come, and he followed me home like a three-year-old. And of course everything was set when we got there. I'd rigged up the settee so it looked like somebody was lying on it under a blanket. I'd even squeezed the blood from half a pound of pig's liver on to the blanket and he fell for it, hook, line and sinker. He ran straight to the settee, yelling at me to call an ambulance, and I nailed him when he went to lift the blanket.

That was Laughing Boy One. A brilliant operation, but I didn't hang about congratulating myself. I tidied up a bit, then it was time to launch Laughing Boy Two. I'd planned to use the same trick in reverse, but when I got to the High Street Link the Stink had gone. I mooched about a bit but there was no sign of him.

Still, never mind, eh? There's always tomorrow. Unless you're Ginger, I mean.

Next day was a Friday, and I spent it looking for Ginger. I tapped a bit as well – had to, or I'd have starved – but all the time I was looking for him and he didn't show. It's happened, I told myself. He's gone back to his real mates, like you always knew he might. I kept hoping though, deep down, and when you're missing someone you keep seeing them. There was this woman – Mrs Chambers – lived next door when I was a kid. When she was about fifty her husband died, and for ages afterwards she kept seeing him on the street or in the supermarket. She'd jump off the bus or abandon her trolley and go chasing after him, and of course it was always somebody else. And that's what it was like for me that Friday. I'd catch a glimpse of somebody across the road or through a shop window – somebody just like Ginger – and when I got close I'd find myself gawping at a stranger. It happened half a dozen times.

Around dusk it started to rain so I went and sat in a doorway on Pratt Street, watching people go in and out of a posh chippy opposite. Normally the smell of the food would have driven me out of my tree, but I guess I was half out of it already. A little voice kept going Ginger, Ginger, like that. It was doing my head in. I thought, what if he's lying in hospital somewhere, unconscious, and nobody knows who he is? He might have walked past the end of this street a minute ago, looking for me. Or maybe he's lost his memory.

In the end, for something to do I got up and trailed

along to the station. There was a guy just inside, selling the paper. He was there a lot and I knew him by sight. I walked past him a couple of times, then went up to him. 'Were you here last night?' I asked.

'Yeah.' He looked at me. 'Why?'

'I – I'm looking for someone. My mate. We were supposed to meet here last night. I wondered if you'd seen him.'

He shrugged. 'I seen a lot of people last night. Hundreds. What's he look like, this mate of yours?'

'Tallish. Red hair. Bit older than me. Carries a green pack. Ginger, they call him.'

'Hmm.' He nodded. 'I might have seen him. There was a guy like that last night. I remember 'cause he was talking to this old feller. Shouting. Something about hospital. They went off together.'

'Which way'd they go?'

'I dunno, do I? Wasn't taking much notice. It might not have been him, anyway.'

'No.' I hesitated. 'Look – will you do me a favour?'

'Depends.'

'If you see him again, will you tell him Link's been asking after him?'

'Link?'

'Yeah.'

'He mentioned Link. The old guy. Link's had an accident. Something like that.'

'But – I'm Link. I haven't had an accident. Are you sure that's what he said?'

'Think so, yeah. The other guy acted sort of frantic – pulling him along, shouting.'

'And you didn't notice which way they went?'

'No, mate. Sorry.'

I hardly slept at all. Thoughts whirled round and round inside my skull and I was hungry as hell. There were loads of parked cars on Pratt Street and people kept coming past, chatting and laughing, banging doors and revving up. I was glad when it started to come light.

I had a coffee in an all-night joint and waited till it was time to go along to the market. I kidded myself I was going for a wash and so on, but really I was hoping he'd be there.

He wasn't, but looking down from the walkway outside the toilets I spotted the girl Ginger had talked to in the caff. She seemed to be by herself this time. I pelted along the walkway and down the steps and found her looking at hats. I touched her sleeve.

'Hi.'

She returned my hi, but I could tell she didn't remember me.

'Link,' I reminded. 'I was with Ginger.'

'Oh, yeah. Where is he?'

'I was hoping you'd tell me.'

She shook her head. 'I haven't seen him since Thursday.'

'Me neither. Was it you he was meeting – in Holborn?'

She nodded. 'Me, Tim and Ricky – the guys you saw before. We meet at the Macklin Street Centre some-times. Didn't he come back here?'

'I dunno.' I told her what the guy in the station had said. She shook her head. 'Ginger doesn't know anyone here 'cept Captain Hook.' She frowned. 'Accident? Hospital? Are you sure the guy wasn't winding you up?'

'Pretty sure.'

She pulled a face. 'Weird-o.'

I looked at her. 'I'm worried, er – I'm sorry, I don't know your name?'

'Toya.' She smiled briefly. 'Well, it's not really, but it's what I like to be called.'

'I'm worried, Toya. I've looked all over. I don't know what to do.'

She shook her head. 'There's nothing you can do, Link. Guys like Ginger come and go, y'know? Move on. Maybe he found work.'

'Hmm.' I looked down, hacking at a muddy banana skin with the toe of my trainer. 'If you see him, will you tell him I've been looking for him?'

She nodded. 'Sure, if I see him, only don't hang by your feet, okay?'

'Thanks.' I had enough dosh for two coffees and meant to offer her one, but she moved off without saying goodbye and I thought, that's the secret. Don't let anybody close. Don't depend on anyone, 'cause they'll only let you down. I turned away. From now on, I told myself, I'll worry about me. Just me. It was a resolution I was to keep for about four minutes.

I went in the caff. The same one as before. I was trying not to look for Ginger, but looking anyway. There was one empty table. I got a coffee and sat down.

The New Me. That's what I was thinking. I don't need anyone. Solo and coping, right? Right.

I nursed the coffee. It was warm in here and raw outside so it paid to stay put. I was halfway down the mug when she walked in.

She was dossing, I could see that, but she was the best looking dosser I'd ever seen. I noticed her hair first. Chestnut, spilling from under her green knitted cap like fire. Her eyes were terrific, too – dark and wide and shining like she'd just had twelve hours' kip. She had on a battered waxed jacket, torn muddy jeans and broken-down trainers, but she soared above her scruffiness – her looks and bearing sort of cancelled it out.

She didn't look at anybody as she crossed the caff, but everybody looked at her. I couldn't tear my eyes away. She got a Coke and turned, looking for somewhere to sit. Her eyes – those fantastic eyes – met mine for a second and I smiled. No chance, I told myself. Scruffy little git like you.

I was wrong. She came over. Every eye in the place followed her. She nodded at one of the three empty chairs. 'Anyone sitting here?' She sounded Scottish. I shook my head.

'Mind if I join you, then?' I nodded, saying nothing. Being the New Me. She unslung her pack, dropped it next to mine and sat down. I lifted my mug and sipped tepid coffee, gazing out the window. I was acting so cool it was unbelievable but that's all it was – acting. In the real world the blood was pounding in my ears and it was as much as I could do to keep from goggling at that fantastic face.

She inserted a straw in her Coke and sucked. When I risked a glance at her she dropped her eyes. I sipped more coffee, sensing her eyes on my face. I mean I could actually feel them, like lasers. After a bit she said, 'Have you been long in London?' Without looking at her I nodded.

'How long?'

'Year, year and a half,' I lied. Well – in five minutes she'd get up and walk away and we'd never meet again.

'That right?' She sounded suitably impressed. 'You'll know your way around, then?'

I shrugged. 'Some.' Man of few words.

'What d'they call you?'

'Link.'

'Link?' She sucked up Coke. 'What's that short for?'

'It's short for I have another name but prefer to be known by this one.'

'Sorry.' She looked sorry. 'I'm Gail.'

'Hi, Gail. Just landed, right?'

'Right.'

'From? Don't tell me if you don't want.'

'Glasgow.'

'Ah-ha. Heavy scene?'

'Aye. Stepfather.'

'Ah – say no more.'

She looked at me. 'You too?'

'Uh-huh.' The New Me. The guy who doesn't let anybody get close and here I am, spilling my guts to the first stranger I meet because she's got nice hair and laser eyes. I drained my mug and pushed back my chair. 'I've gotta go.'

'Why?' She looked crestfallen. I shrugged.

'Things to do.' I stood up. This was costing me, but I wasn't going to wind up watching trains for her to come back.

'Don't go.' So simple. So direct. Something hot and heavy stirred in my chest. I hesitated, dangling my pack, looking down at her. 'What d'you want, Gail?'

Her eyes held mine. 'I'm scared, Link,' she murmured. 'I don't know what to do – how to live on the street.'

'You learn, Gail. That's all.' Oh yeah? sneered a voice inside my head. What about your dependence on Ginger, then – that urge to cling? It came to me that this was the first time I'd thought of Ginger since she walked in, and that was powerful medicine. Maybe we needed each other. I dropped my pack and sat down.

Oh dear, oh dear. Link the Stink's in love and Laughing Boy Two's up shit creek.

Yesterday – that's Friday – I made a mistake. A gross error, like Hitler's invasion of Russia. If I'd concentrated on Link I might have had him, but I didn't. Instead I went looking for boots. Reconditioned Army boots.

Not for me. Oh, no. My marching days are over, as you know. These were for my army. The Camden Horizontals, as I've christened 'em. Four pairs I needed, all different sizes, and I got 'em, too, in Bethnal Green. 'Course they're not a perfect fit, none of 'em, but then they don't need to be. My lads'll not be doing a lot of yomping, so it doesn't matter if the footwear's a bit slack or a bit snug. All it has to do is shine, and it does.

Anyway, I lost my chance yesterday, and when I picked up his trail this morning he bumped into some tart in a caff up the market and they left together, so it's not going to be easy. I'll have to fall back. Re-group. Devise fresh tactics. And I'm the feller who can do it. By golly I am.

We hit it off, Gail and me, from the word go. She got me another coffee and we sat there talking, oblivious to everything around us. It was unbelievable. When you're homeless and hungry you're an outsider. Normal everyday experience doesn't apply to you. You know – things like having a job to go to, mates to meet, a motor bike to save up for. You don't buy CDs or get your hair cut or have dental check-ups or shop for clothes. You can't. Your circumstances put those sorts of things beyond your reach. To all intents and purposes you belong to a separate species, and one of the hardest bits is how it cuts you off from girls. If you're a guy, I mean. See – normally a young bloke sees a girl passing by and he'll smile and maybe call out something to her. Chat her up a bit. It doesn't mean anything and it won't usually lead to anything – it's just part of being young and on the loose if you know what I mean. And now and then – maybe one time in a hundred – it does lead to something and you've got a relationship which might or might not last. The important thing is that you're part of it, right? One of the guys. Or one of the girls. But if you're dossing, you're not. You try chatting up a girl when you're ragged and grimy and pasty-faced and your teeth are crummy and she knows you don't even have the price of a coffee. No chance. Not only will you not get off with her, you won't even get the smile. A dirty look and a wide berth's more like it. And the same in reverse if you're a girl, I guess. After a bit you start thinking of yourself as a different creature – a creature that lives beside ordinary people but isn't one of them.

So finding myself suddenly sitting in this caff, chatting with a fantastic-looking girl, felt really strange. For the first time in months I wasn't some sort of freak. I was just a young guy getting to know a girl, like people do. I forgot my tatty clothes and matted hair and the ache in my gut. I forgot about cold, hard doorways and cold, hard eyes and the fact that I couldn't even invite her to see a movie. I was a guy, she was a girl and I might be falling in love. That was all I knew. All I wanted to know. I didn't even notice we'd left the caff till I found myself sitting on a wall in weak sunshine, holding her hand while some old geezer passing by frowned at us like we were committing a crime or something. It was the start of a brilliant time for me, and all I can say is it's a good job we can't see into the future.

So we're sitting on this wall and she says, 'Let's get chips and eat them by the water.' It's a warm day for February at that, but there's one snag. 'I got no dosh,' I tell her.

'I have.'

'Yeah, but it's gotta last. It's slim pickings, tapping.'

'I got plenty,' she says.

'You won't have for long if you broadcast it like that.' I grin. 'How d'you know I won't mug you for it?'

'Try it,' she says. 'You'll mebbe get something you didn't bargain for.'

She bought chips and we sat by the water. I said, 'What you dossing for if you got dosh – you could get a place.'

She shrugged. 'Like you said, it's gotta last. And anyway, I'm with you now. I don't need a place.'

This sounded reasonable as well as flattering and I accepted it. I should've pushed a bit harder but I was well in love by this time and you don't, do you?

We ate and talked. She was terminally curious about what she called The Scene – she meant life on the street. She asked about a million questions and I did my best to answer them. I had no choice, since I'd passed myself off to her as an old hand. To be perfectly honest I was beginning to regret having lied – not because of the questions, but because of love, I suppose – which is ironic considering what happened later, but this was now.

I didn't tap at all that day. Neither of us did. We strolled through the market, looking at the costly junk and the punters who were buying it. We got Cokes and even ate again, though my wizened gut wasn't hungry. I don't believe I thought of Ginger once, except when I was telling her about him, which is rotten, but shows what love will do. And so the day slipped by.

I'd told her about Captain Hook, and when it got dark I thought of suggesting a night on board, but I didn't. For one thing it'd have seemed cheeky when it was her dosh, and for another I didn't want us to spend our first night in a reeking crowd. I wanted Gail to myself, so I took her to a favourite doorway of mine where we bedded down for the night.

Nothing happened. Sorry to disappoint, but it's true. I don't know why. Malnutrition perhaps, or stepfathers. All we seemed to want was to sleep with our arms round each other, and that's what we did. But if you think that must've been dead boring, you're wrong.

* * *

73

Sunday she wanted to try her hand at tapping so we rode down to Charing Cross. I remembered how Ginger had started me off – leaving me by the National Gallery while he did Trafalgar Square, and we did the same. I didn't want to leave her, even though we'd be practically in sight of each other. It was a cold morning but dry, and there were quite a lot of people about. As I made the round of benches, a little video kept playing itself inside my head. I was the star. The opening scene showed me going across to collect Gail in a couple of hours' time and finding she's vanished. After that came a succession of shots of me in various stressful situations. Running through unfamiliar streets, calling her name. Trying to interest the police who don't want to know. Waiting on Camden Station forever. I tried to suppress this video, reminding myself that it was Gail who'd wanted us to stick together, so she was hardly likely to do a runner the minute my back was turned, but it was no use. I guess I was still haunted by the way Ginger had dropped out of my life. Anyway, I didn't stick it long. The pigeons were doing better than I was in any case – scoring chunks of bread and handfuls of corn while I got sweet FA. I swear if I ever come to London again I'll come as a pigeon. I did about half an hour then started making my way back, tapping all the way.

She wasn't there. Not on the steps, not on the pavement. Panic squeezed my heart. I ran up the steps and looked all round, then set off along the front of the Gallery. I'd just turned into St Martin's Place when I saw her coming out of a phone box. My relief was so overwhelming that it was some time before it occurred to me to wonder whom she'd been calling. When I asked she said, 'My sister in Glasgow. She made me promise to keep in touch.'

It sounded totally feasible. I nodded. 'I've got a sister. Carole. I don't phone though – clean break, y'know?'

'Hmm.' She nodded. 'I promised.'

'Oh, I'm not getting at you. I only –'

'I know.' She squeezed my hand.

I grinned, squeezing hers. 'How much did you make?'

She shrugged. 'Dunno. Never counted. Hang on.' She dug in her pockets, produced a double handful of change and counted it. 'Two pounds thirty.' She pocketed the coins. 'How about you?'

I shook my head. 'Twelve pence, and I'm supposed to be the expert.'

'Beginner's luck,' she smiled. 'Or maybe it's because I'm a woman.' She gazed at me. 'Anyway, we share, don't we – everything?'

And from then on we did, and it was all so fantastic that time just flew. I practically stopped noticing the cold. When something happened to jerk me back into the real world, it was spring.

You mustn't think I've been idle, just because Link the Stink continues to evade me. A peek under the famous floorboards is all you'd need to convince you of my continuing determination to rid my country of the riff-raff that's dragging it down.

My tally of recruits now stands at seven. Seven! Oh, I know I went on a bit when we reached three and three *is* a significant number, but seven – seven's what you call a mystical number, the reason being one that need not detain us. All I know is, lots of things go in sevens, like the seven deadly sins and the seventh son of a seventh son, not to mention the days of the week and *The Magnificent Seven*.

I got a black one, which goes to show there's no racial discrimination in the Camden Horizontals. It also helps break up the pattern – the deadly pattern I mentioned earlier. You can just imagine it, can't you – some smart-ass Detective Constable looking for a pattern, saying, all his victims have been white – *that* could be significant. Well it ain't, so there! There is no pattern, except that each operation has been a text-book example of brilliance, and they'll never see that.

They've bags of swank, my lads. Shiny boots and nice short hair. And if you think the boots'll give me away – if you're thinking the fella I get 'em off must be starting to wonder – forget it. I don't go to one fella. I go to three. So far. And there'll be more yet, by golly there will. You don't catch old Shelter that easily.

So the business continues. Volunteers swell the ranks. And they *are* volunteers, you know – nobody forces 'em to come. They come for what recruits have always come for – an end to hunger and a roof over their heads, and they get it. None of my lads is hungry, and they've got a roof over their heads and a floor as well. I sometimes think I spoil 'em.

Where was I? Oh, yes – spring, and the real world.

It was magic being with Gail. Like I said, I seemed to stop noticing the cold, and tapping became a sort of game for us – a contest to see who could score most. It wasn't heavy – I don't mean that. It was a light-hearted game – I never minded when Gail won, which she often did.

Mind you, the situation had its drawbacks. For a start I got jealous of Gail. Possessive, I suppose. I hated letting her out of my sight. She was so good-looking I was terrified some guy'd come along – someone with a job and a car and a place to live, maybe – and snatch her away. Well – it'd be no contest would it? And that was the other drawback. I started wanting work so I could offer her a home. I'd always wanted a job of course, but now it became a longing – almost an obsession. Worst thing was, I knew it was a non-starter – nobody was going to give me a chance the way I looked now – but it didn't stop me wanting, or trying. I really did try, too. I haunted the Job Centre, wrote letters on nicked paper, bought stamps I couldn't afford – I even had a couple of interviews but I never got a result. They know, you see. If you have to give some job club as a return address, they know you've nowhere to live. They know you haven't worked in a long time – maybe never, and they don't want to know. They've so many applicants to choose from, why should they take on a dosser? I wouldn't, if I was in their shoes.

It was torture too, because every time I went chasing after a prospect it meant leaving her behind, and all the time I was gone I'd be worrying. Maybe that's one reason I never got anything – they could tell I hadn't brought my brain with me. Anyway, April came along and my situation hadn't changed and Gail was still with me, which astonished me when I allowed myself to think about it. She didn't seem to mind that I had nothing to offer. I put it down to love.

One Saturday – it was a warm, sunny day – we were sitting on the tow-path opposite Pullit, the local night-spot, enjoying the sunshine, when a middle-aged guy came up to us. 'Excuse me,' he said. 'I wonder if you can help me?' I thought he must be lost or something, but then he said, 'I'm trying to trace my daughter, and I wondered if you might have seen her. Her name's Tanya. This is her.' He held out a snapshot. Gail took it, shook her head and passed it to me. It was Toya. I nodded. 'I've seen her a couple of times.'

'Where?' The guy practically jumped down my throat. 'Where'd you see her? When?'

I nodded towards the Lock. 'There. The market. Not for a while, though.'

'Did you talk to her? Did she say where she was living or anything like that?'

I shook my head. 'She was dossing, I think. I don't know where she hangs out.'

'Was she with anyone – an older man, perhaps?'

'No. Once she was with two young guys, the other time she was alone.' I looked at him. 'Why would she be with an older man?'

He shook his head. When he spoke I could tell he was trying to keep from crying. 'I don't know. I spoke to a man last night – a man in a watchman's hut. He told me he might have seen my daughter about a week ago, going into the ground floor flat of the house he lives in, with the man who has the flat. A man in his forties.'

'Did he give you the address? Have you tried there?' I knew his informant must be Captain Hook. He nodded. 'I went there last night. I rang the bell but there was nobody in.'

'The guy in the watchman's hut – does he know this man?'

'No. He's not been there long, apparently.'

'Have you tried the police?'

'No. I tried them months ago – when Tanya left home. They didn't want to know. She's seventeen, you see – free to go where she chooses.' He stifled a sob. 'It's breaking her mother's heart.'

Poor sods, I thought. They drive their kid out, probably without meaning to, then think tramping round London with a snapshot'll get her back. It won't, but I wish someone cared about me like that.

'Look,' I said. 'We'll look out for your daughter, and if we see her we'll say we saw you – get her to phone home, okay?'

He was so grateful he practically hugged me. 'Bless you,' he says, shoving a fiver in my unresisting hand. 'Bless you both.'

He shambled off, clutching his snapshot and his useless hope. Gail and I watched him go, each pretending not to notice how close the other was to tears.

Daily Routine Orders 14

Fella rang my bell last night. 22.00 hours. I wasn't worried. Provided you've got the situation under control there's nothing to worry about. A swift recce through the curtain showed me a shortish chap of about forty-five. It was too dark for me to see his features, but something about the way he was standing told me he was agitated so I judged it best not to reveal my position. I never show a strong light after dusk. My table lamp has a sixty-watt bulb and from outside, with the curtains drawn, no illumination is visible. I know this because I've checked. Always check everything, that's my golden rule. So I lay low and waited. He tried twice more, then left. I don't know who he was or what he wanted, but instinct warns me he could be related to one of my recruits. I might be wrong, but my instincts are usually pretty sharp so I'll exercise particular care over the next day or so.

By golly I will.

We'd probably have thought no more about it if it hadn't been for Nick. I mean, Captain Hook might easily have been mistaken, and people move on all the time. I'd have forgotten Toya even quicker than I forgot Ginger if we hadn't run into Nick that same afternoon, and who knows what might have happened then?

Nick's the guy who sells *The Big Issue* on Camden Station, but we came across him under the bridge on the High Street. I'd just tapped a Yank for a quid when he came up to me. 'I'm glad I saw you,' he said. 'Something funny's just happened.'

'Don't tell me,' I said. 'The Prime Minister's offered you a kip at Number Ten, right?'

'No, listen. You know when you were looking for that mate of yours a while back?'

'Ginger. Yeah?'

'Well, I told you I saw him leave the station with an older guy, didn't I?'

'Yes.' An older guy. Now where had I heard that recently?

'Well, this morning an old gimmer comes up to me with a photo of his daughter, asking if I've seen her.'

I nodded. 'We saw him too. What about it?'

'This about it, my old mate. I *did* see her, a few days back, leaving the station with the same guy your mucker went off with.'

I looked at him. 'What're you saying? You mean, they go off with this guy –'

82

'And vanish. Dodgy, or what?'

'Yeah. Dodgy. Did you tell the old guy?'

'Sure. He said somebody else saw the lass with a man, going into a house.'

'I know. It was Captain Hook. His flat's in the house. The guy's been there but nobody answered the door. Did you tell him to go to the cops?'

'Naw. No point, is there? All they'd say is, dossers move on all the time. No evidence, see? Nothing concrete.'

'Yeah, but –'

'I know. We could be talking murder here. Double murder, but it's all supposition, my old mate.'

'So what do we do?'

Nick shrugged. 'I know what he looks like, and the gallant Captain has the address. I suggest we watch him for a bit – see what he does. If he's what we think he is he's bound to give himself away. Then we tell the fuzz.'

'And what if he takes some other kid home in the meantime – we can't watch him twenty-four hours a day.' I looked at Gail. 'What do you reckon, Gail?'

'I – I'm not sure, Link. Listen – I've got to make a phone call. My sister. I'll see you outside the Brazilia in ten minutes and we'll talk about it, okay?'

We watched her cross the street. Nick grinned. 'Now that's what I call a cool chick. We tell her there's probably a killer stalking the streets and she goes off to phone her sister. I don't know where you find 'em, Link old son.' He punched my arm. 'I'll see you.'

The afternoon was warm, the pavements thronged with sightseers. I strolled along to the Brazilia and leaned against the wall with my eyes closed, enjoying the sun on my face. If I'd known then what I know now, it would've spoiled my whole day.

* * *

When Gail got back I said, 'We should go to the fuzz.' I'd been thinking about Ginger. The sort of guy he was. He wouldn't have just gone off without saying anything. I'd half convinced myself he'd done exactly that because there'd been no other explanation, but now –

'Can if you like,' said Gail. 'But I doubt if they'll be impressed.'

We went up to Albany Street and they weren't impressed. In fact it took us all our time to get past the front desk. Eventually a Detective Sergeant came. Detective Sergeant Ireson. He took us into a cubicle. I started to tell him about Ginger but he interrupted. 'I should tell you that following representations by a member of the public, the matter you're concerned about was investigated. Nothing was found, and no further action is contemplated.'

'No further – did you *talk* to the guy? Did you ask him what he was doing with my mate? With this Tanya?'

The Sergeant looked irritated. 'All normal procedures were followed,' he growled. 'Nothing was found to justify further action so the matter is officially closed. And now if you'll excuse me, I have a job to do.'

'But what did the guy *say*?'

'G'day, sir.'

Ha, ha, ha. Ha, ha, ha, ha, ha, ha, ha! That's the sound of Shelter having the last laugh, and no wonder. The enemy has attacked in strength and has been repulsed.

I'd just got back from buying boots and was feeding the damn cat when they arrived. Two officers in an Escort. One male, one female. I considered not answering the door but then I thought, why not? This was bound to happen eventually. Confront the enemy, Shelter old lad. No retreat. No surrender.

I was magnificent. Stowed my purchases in the cupboard. Smiled on the step, invited 'em in, offered coffee which they declined. How could I be of help? We're making inquiries about a young woman, they said. This woman. They pushed a snapshot at me, suddenly, hoping I'd flinch or something – give myself away. Not a chance. 'Oh, yes,' I said, cool as a cucumber. 'We've met. In fact she was here, in this very flat, just the other day. A week last Tuesday, to be precise.'

Well, of course they wanted to know *why* she'd been here – under what circumstances, at which point I went all shy and modest. 'Ah, well,' I said. 'You see, I'm lucky enough to be quite comfortably off. I have money in the bank and a good pension, and I feel terribly sorry for those unfortunate young persons one sees sleeping out of doors in cardboard boxes and so forth, so now and then I – I invite one of them back here for a bath and a hot meal. I never let them stay overnight because – well – because I'm afraid I might be murdered in my bed, I suppose, but I usually give them a pound or two to help them on their way.' At this point I shrugged and gave them my daftest grin. 'It's silly, I know, but it makes me feel better.'

'It could be dangerous, sir, in all sorts of ways.'

'I know, officer, but –' The stupid grin again.

'So you fed this young woman and gave her money?'

'Yes.'

'Did you talk to her, sir – did she mention going away at all?'

I shook my head. 'They tend not to talk about themselves, Inspector, and I don't pry.' He was a constable but I addressed him as inspector.

'Of course not, sir. What time of day was it when she left the house?'

'It was evening. Late evening. Tennish, ten thirty. It was raining.' I did my rueful smile. 'I hate to turn 'em out, but as I said –'

'Quite, sir. And she didn't say where she was going?'

'No.' I'd practised the concerned frown and I employed it now. 'I do hope nothing terrible's befallen her, Inspector. She was a charming girl – charming.'

'Yes, sir. From a good home, I believe.' They moved towards the door 'We won't take up any more of your time, sir. Thanks for your help – and do be careful who you bring into your home. Some of 'em are dead wrong 'uns, y'know.'

'I know, Inspector. I'll be careful.'

I stood in the doorway with the bloody cat in my arms. When they were half-way down the path I called after them. 'Will you let me know if – you know – if she turns up?'

'Of course, sir. G'night, sir.'

'Good night, Inspector. Good night, Sergeant.'

Ha, ha, ha. Ha, ha, ha, ha, ha!

'So now what do we do?' We were walking back up Parkway. The sun was going down. Gail shrugged. 'What Nick suggested, I suppose. Keep an eye on this chap – hope he slips up.'

'I think we should warn people. You know – don't go off with anyone.'

'Hmm. You'd think they'd know that anyway. One thing we need to know is what he looks like.'

I nodded. 'We'll get Nick to point him out on Monday.'

'Why not now, or tomorrow?'

I shook my head. 'He won't be around. Nick, I mean. He lives in a squat, but I don't know where.'

'We could try and spot the guy ourselves – get the address from Captain Hook.'

I scoffed. 'He won't give it. It's his own address, Gail. He'd think we were planning to do his place over.'

She grinned. 'I think he'll tell me, if I'm by myself. You take my pack and wait here.'

I waited on the canal bridge. It was dusk and turning a bit nippy. I shivered, and it wasn't just the cold. I was thinking about Ginger, and Tanya who liked to be called Toya, and her dad who said bless you and shoved a fiver in my hand. I was thinking about Gail, too – how she'd changed my life for the better, but how, whenever I thought of her, a faint unease would stir somewhere deep inside – a sensation I strove to smother or ignore. A cool chick, Nick had called her, but it wasn't quite that. She was cool, but there was something else – a sort of poise; a self-possession which jarred with her circumstances. It seems a funny thing to say, but she wasn't screwed up enough. I must have known, too, deep down, but I kept shoving it away. If it was a dream it was a warm dream, and I didn't want to wake.

She was back in a few minutes, smiling. 'Nine Mornington Place,' she chirped, shouldering her pack. I nodded but didn't say anything and we set off along the High Street.

It was a biggish, three-storey house in a short Victorian terrace. There was a minute, sour-looking front garden in which three dustbins took up most of the space. There was no gate. A short path led from the gateway to the white door. No light showed in any of the windows.

'Nobody home,' said Gail. We were standing in the shadow of some budding sycamores across the street.

'Let's hang about a bit,' I murmured. Looking at the place made me shiver. The video inside my skull came on, and I saw Ginger following a shadowy figure up to that white door. Is that how it happened, I wondered. When, exactly? Where was I at that moment? and *why* had Ginger followed him – Ginger and Toya and possibly others. Why?

Gail had a watch. We waited forty-five minutes. Nobody went in, nobody came out. A woman kept coming to a lighted upstairs window next door, seeming to look straight at us. She probably couldn't even see us, but it made us nervous. If you're homeless it's not smart to be found loitering in a residential area, especially after dark, and she just might phone the police. 'Come on,' I said. 'We'll try again tomorrow.'

* * *

Sunday we were back under the sycamores by half eight. It was dry but the sun was still behind the houses so it was nippy, too. All the curtains were closed at number nine. I wished me and Gail were having a lie-in like the bastards in those rooms. A good night's sleep in a comfy bed, a lie-in till about ten and a breakfast of eggs and bacon, toast and coffee, eaten slowly in a warm kitchen. Paradise, and millions take it completely for granted.

Our man, if it was our man, didn't lie in till ten. Just before nine the door opened a crack and a black and white cat shot out, followed by a hand. This hand groped for the pint of milk on the doorstep, found it and pulled it in through the crack. The door closed, and a minute later the downstairs curtains opened. Gail and I took a stroll along the road and watched from the corner. After about ten minutes a guy came out, closing the door behind him. He was a big man in his forties. He wore an Aran sweater and cord trousers and had very short sandy hair. As he came down the path the cat, which had been sitting on the wall, jumped down and fled. The man turned left and strode off along the street.

'What d'you want to do?' said Gail. 'Follow?'

'Naw. He's not going far. Not dressed for it. Probably off for a paper.'

I was right. He was back in five minutes with a thickish roll of Sunday reading tucked under his arm. He turned into the gateway without noticing us and let himself into the house with a latchkey.

'D'you reckon that's our man, then?'

Gail shrugged. 'Well, it wasn't Captain Hook, and he seems to live on the ground floor, so I'd say yes, that's our man.'

'But he looks so – ordinary.'

'He might *be* ordinary, Link. We don't *know* he's done anything, do we? The police found nothing suspicious.'

'We know he was seen with Ginger and Toya,' I said. 'Just before they disappeared. And I know I'd give my left arm for a look inside that house.'

Gail nodded. 'Me too, but it's not possible. All we can do is watch.'

So we watched. We saw the cat return and sit there where the milk bottle had been. We didn't see the upstairs curtains open, but when we sauntered by on the other side at half nine they were open. The sun had cleared the housetops and we strolled in watery sunshine under the trees. We didn't like to stand in one place too long in case we drew attention to ourselves, and there's a limit to the number of times you can walk up and down the same short street without somebody noticing. It was dead boring, anyway, and it didn't look as though our man was coming out, so at a quarter past ten we decided to pack it in till evening. The cat was still on the step when we left.

It was the business with the cat that fooled me. You can say what you like but there's something reassuring about a cat. I mean, say you saw some guy fussing with his cat – fondling it and talking to it and chuckling over it – you wouldn't think, oh-oh – there goes a dangerous man. There goes a killer. I better steer clear of him. Well, you wouldn't, would you? You'd probably think, look at him, the great soft lump. Well, anyway, that's my excuse for what happened to me that evening, but I guess I'd better start at the beginning.

First off, there was the rain. It'd been a lovely morning – sunny and warm – but around twelve it clouded over and began to pour. Gail and I were tapping along the High Street when it started, so all we did was move under the rail bridge and carry on. The weather didn't seem to deter the punters – the market was seething as usual and we did all right, but it was the rain that led to our fight.

We never fought, Gail and me. We felt the same way about most things and so we got along fine. But when it started to get dark that Sunday evening and I suggested it was time to get back to Mornington Place, she said, 'Not me – not in this stuff.'

'What stuff?' I cried. 'What you on about, Gail?'

'The rain, dummy. I'm not standing in the rain till God knows what time, waiting for some dumbo who'll probably decide to stay home and keep dry.'

'But we agreed. We said we'd go back tonight.'

'It wasn't raining then. And anyway I've got a couple of things to see to.'

'Like what? Phoning your sister? Again? We'd both eat better if you didn't shove so much dosh in the damn phone.'

'It's my dosh, Link. I can do what I like with it, and anyway I'm not phoning my sister. I've other things to do.'

'And they're none of my business, right?'

'Right.'

'Well, shove off and do 'em then, only don't expect me to hang around like I'm your dog or something till you decide to come back. I'll be in Mornington Place if you want me.'

And that's how I came to be alone in Mornington Place when the cat business happened.

It was a miserable vigil. Miserable. I was even more down than when Ginger disappeared. I stood under the dripping trees – they weren't in leaf enough to keep the rain out – and thought about Gail. I hadn't meant for

91

us to fight. I loved her. It was just that I'd spent all day thinking about Ginger and Toya and Nine Mornington Place. I saw a movie once – Ten Rillington Place – about this sick killer who lured women into his house and murdered them. It was a true story. The title – Ten Rillington Place – had a ring to it, and in my imagination Nine Mornington Place was beginning to have that same ring. I'd more or less convinced myself that horrible things had been done in that house, and that it was down to me to expose them.

I don't know what time it was when the door opened. I seemed to have been there hours. I was soaked and freezing, and I'd more or less decided to jack it in and go make it up with Gail when suddenly there he was – the guy we'd been watching that morning. The very ordinary guy who wore cords and kept a moggy and liked to read the Sunday papers. He was standing on the doorstep, silhouetted against the dim light which spilled through the doorway. He was calling softly, 'Sappho – chi-chi-chi – here, Sappho.' I stood absolutely still, way back under the sycamores. He was obviously calling a cat – probably the one we'd seen earlier – but no cat appeared. After a minute or so the guy went inside, leaving the door ajar. I watched the strip of light, and in a moment he reappeared carrying a dish. He squatted and put the dish on the step. 'Sappho!' he called, striking the dish gently with a fork or spoon. 'C'mon Sappho – meat.' He was in shirt-sleeves and must have felt cold, but he persisted, calling and calling, but no cat appeared. Presently he straightened up and came shuffling down to the gateway in carpet slippers with a fork in his hand, peering to left and right, calling. I thought, this is your monster? Your serial killer? A guy who'll stand in shirt-sleeves in the rain, calling his cat? Aw, come *on*! It was then he spotted me.

I knew he'd seen me and I wasn't scared – what's scary about a guy who can't find his pussycat? Embarrassed is what I was. Embarrassed, because it must've been obvious I'd been watching him. I started to move away but he called out, 'I say – excuse me?'

I looked across. 'Me?'

'Y – yes. You haven't by any chance seen a cat, have you? A black and white cat?'

I shook my head.

'Oh. Pity. She hates the rain, you see. Detests it. I felt sure she'd be waiting on the step, especially since it's her suppertime. I do hope nothing's –' He broke off and looked at me. 'Oh, I say – I am most terribly sorry.' He looked sorry. 'Here am I, fussing about a silly cat and there you are, soaked to the skin. I – have you nowhere to go, young man?'

I shook my head.

'That's terrible. Terrible.' He stood looking at me, fiddling with the fork. I could tell he didn't know what to say.

'I'll be off then,' I mumbled.

'Yes.' He nodded, but continued to stare. As I turned away he said, 'I suppose you're hungry?'

'I'm all right.' I'd started to walk away – would have got clear away if the cat hadn't appeared at that moment, scampering under a streetlamp.

'Sappho!' I turned. The creature ran to him and he lifted it. Cradled it in his arms, crooning. Rocked it like a baby, burying his face in its wet fur, oblivious to the rain which was drenching him, the great soft noodle. And to think – I turned away.

'Young man?'

'Huh?'

'Can I offer you something to eat or – I dunno – a couple of quid?' He dithered, anxious to do something for me but worried his offer might offend. 'There's a coat – a good one – I don't use anymore. You're welcome to that if it'll help.'

I wasn't hungry but I was cold and wet and the coat sounded tempting. I nodded. 'That coat'll be – thanks.' He smiled and began shuffling back to the house, cradling the cat. I followed. It was as simple as that.

There was a short hallway with a door on the right and stairs at the end. The guy pushed open the door with his free hand and stood aside, holding the cat. 'Go on in, young man. I'll be with you in a jiffy.'

The room smelled of polish and was so tidy it looked like nobody used it. Heavy curtains covered the bay window. The only light came from a lamp which stood on a gleaming table. I stood dripping on the guy's immaculate carpet while he carried Sappho through to what I assumed was the kitchen. After a moment he called out, 'You couldn't fetch the dish, could you – the one on the step?'

'Sure.'

'You don't mind?' He chuckled. 'I sometimes think I'd forget my head if it was loose.'

I retrieved the dish with its little heap of mush and carried it through to the kitchen. He had the cat swaddled in a pink towel. 'Thanks.' He smiled. 'Thanks a lot. Just put it down anywhere. I'll get the coat in a minute.'

I went back into the other room, conscious of leaving wet footprints. If I'd entertained lingering suspicions on entering the house they'd now dissolved. The man was obviously a total wally with his cat and his obsessive tidiness. I couldn't help smiling to myself as I surveyed the room. Plumped cushions. Straight pictures. Gleaming surfaces. A place for everything and everything in its place. The occupant of this room was what my grandad used to call a Mary Ellen – the sort of man who wears frilly aprons around the house and may be seen in the garden, pegging out clothes. I was getting more complacent by the second till I saw my watch on the sideboard.

It was mine, all right. The one I'd handed over to the Scouser about a million years ago. I'd have known it anywhere. There was a tightening sensation in my chest as I stepped over for a closer look, and when the door slammed I cried out.

He'd come in without my hearing. Crossed the room. Was standing now with his broad back against the door, smiling a different smile. He nodded towards the sideboard. 'That was – careless of me.' He chuckled, and it was not a wally's chuckle. 'Still, it doesn't matter, does it – not now.' He looked at me and hissed, 'Link. Link the Stink. Laughing Boy Two, at last. Whassamatter, Laughing Boy – cat gotcha tongue?' He laughed and called towards the kitchen, 'Hey Sappho – got the kid's tongue, have you?'

I stared at the guy, paralysed with horror. We'd been right, Gail and Nick and me. This was our man. You only had to look in his eyes to know he was mad. He was totally out of his tree and he had me trapped, like Toya and Ginger and –

'Oh, yes.' He'd read my mind. 'He's here, the big Liverpudlian, along with the others, and a promising recruit he's turning out to be, too. Lots of potential. Bags and bags of swank. Would you like to see?'

'No!' It came out as a shriek. I pressed myself against the sideboard. 'I want to go home. Let me go.'

He laughed again, shaking his cropped sandy head. 'Oh no, lad. No going home. Not anymore. You made me wait a long time, but you're in the Army now. The

Camden Horizontals. Come and meet your comrades.'

'Let me go!' I knew it was no use, of course I did, but my brain had packed up. I didn't seem to be able to say anything else. He'd gone down on one knee and was lifting a corner of the carpet. I measured the distance to the window. If I could reach it – smash a pane, I thought –

'Here – have a gander.' He'd folded back the carpet and removed three or four short boards from the floor. 'I'll put the big light on so you can see better.' He got up. As he moved towards the switch by the door I made a dash for the window. The light came on. I grabbed for the drapes as he whirled with an oath, coming for me. I wrapped my arms round the curtains and swung on them. There was a creaking, splintering noise as the rail tore loose at one end and swathes of heavy fabric came down on both of us. Sobbing with terror I clawed myself free, slipped my pack and swung it at the window. The pane cracked but failed to shatter, and before I could take a second swing he was on me.

The strength of the insane. I'd come across that phrase, and now I found out what it meant. I'm not a small guy and he was a lot older but I couldn't break free. I bucked and writhed and lashed out with my feet, but he'd wrapped his arms round me and his grip was like bands of steel. My feet left the floor and he carried me across the room like he'd carried the cat, except he didn't croon or nuzzle, and when we reached the hole in the floor he threw me down and fell on me like a wrestler. I was pinned, lying on my stomach with my head overhanging the hole. A draught rose from the hole, carrying a cloying, sweetish smell. After a few seconds my eyes adjusted to the dimness and I saw them.

There were seven, laid out in a row like sardines. He'd done something to their heads – they were all like his – you couldn't tell if they were girls or boys – but I recognized Ginger by his clothes. His face was – well, I wouldn't have known him from that. I gagged, twisting my head to one side. 'Let me up!' I screamed. 'I'm gonna puke.'

He laughed, 'Puke away, soldier. You're the one'll lie in it, not me.'

I vomited into the horrible grey dust and he laughed again. 'Get it all up,' he roared. 'It'll do you good.' His weight bore down on me so I couldn't breathe. Black shapes floated in front of my eyes. I was losing consciousness.

'Gerroff me!' I gasped. 'I'm passing out.'

'That's the general idea, Link,' he hissed. 'This is your passing-out parade.' He laughed wildly. 'Passing-out parade – geddit?'

He was killing me, slowly, asphyxiation. My mouth yawned as I strove to suck in enough foul air for one last try. 'They know I'm here,' I croaked. 'My friends know I'm here.'

I don't suppose he believed me – he'd know a dying man'll say anything – but my words must have reminded him about the brightly lit room, the curtainless bay, and they saved my life. He swore and lifted himself off me. I heard him scrambling to his feet. Gasping and choking I rolled clear of the hole, knowing I had only seconds to clear my head. The big light went out and in the glow from the small one I saw him returning with bared teeth and a length of flex stretched taut between his fists. I tried to get up but my legs were useless and I fell back and lay, shielding my throat with my hands. He was bending over me, brandishing his garrotte, when the siren screamed.

*   *   *

97

He was yelling at his lads to stand and fight as the coppers dragged him out. I was so dazed I didn't know what was happening. I staggered into the hallway. They'd smashed both doors to get to us. Gail was on the step, trying to get past two policemen. When she saw me she gasped, 'Link – thank God!' The coppers let me through and we flung our arms round each other.

I know exactly what you're thinking. Here comes the happy ending, right? Hang on a minute.

'Was it you?' I asked. 'Did you bring the law?'

She nodded. 'I came looking for you but you weren't around. I was just leaving when the light came on and the curtain fell and I could see you struggling with – him. I knew I couldn't do anything alone so I ran to Albany Street.'

'But – how'd you get 'em to – they wouldn't believe us before. How'd you manage – '

'Link.' She sort of stiffened in my arms. Started to pull away. 'There's something I have to tell you.'

She never told me, though. She didn't have to. They'd finally got the crazy guy into the van. It pulled away with two cars following, and then this poncy-looking dude came through the gateway carrying a fancy camera and all the gear. He pranced up the path grinning like a baboon.

'Louise, darling,' he burbled. 'You're a genius.'

Gail had broken our clinch. I looked around for Louise darling, but there was only me and Gail and the two coppers, and neither of them looked like a Louise. Then it hit me. The guy was talking to Gail.

She'd a sheepish look about her, I'll give her that. 'Link,' she murmured. 'This is Gavin. Gavin – this is the boy I told you about.' Gavin beamed and stuck out a paw. I ignored it and turned to Gail. 'And you,' I blurted. 'Who are you?'

She flushed. 'I'm sorry, Link. My name's Louise Bain. I'm a journalist. I've been –'

'Don't tell me. You've been on to this loony for months, right? But you didn't give a shit how many kids got murdered, just so long as you and this wally were on the spot when they grabbed him.'

'Hey, steady on!' cried the photographer. 'She saved your life, remember.'

I looked at him. 'One more word out of you and I'll ram that fozzing camera right where the sun don't shine.'

Gail was shaking her head. 'You've got it wrong, Link. I was researching homelessness, that's all. I knew nothing about this other business. Nothing at all. You've got to believe me.'

There was more in the same vein. I was so distracted with anger and grief I hardly knew what I was saying. I remember asking Gavin why he didn't get some shots of the victims and sell them to the parents. Gail was in tears by this time, and so was I. It ended with her shoving a wad of banknotes in my hand. 'Good luck, Link,' she choked. 'I'm really sorry.' Gavin was starting his car. She got in with him and I found myself standing in a haze of blue smoke, watching her exit my life.

Oh, I know. I ought to have chucked the money in her face. A telly hero would have, but then a telly hero doesn't have to live on the street. Anyway, that's the sort of happy ending it was.

Yeah, but like – justice was done, right? Was it, though? Shelter (that's what he called himself – they found a sort of log book) – Shelter gets life, which means he gets a roof, a bed and three square meals a day. I don't.

What I hope is this. I hope when Louise and Gavin do their story it'll have some truth in it and that a lot of people will read it. People can only start to make things better if they know what's going on. There *has* to be an end to this some day. I just hope it happens while I'm still around.

In the meantime, though, I'm not sure what I'll do. I can't stay round Camden, that's for sure. Too many ghosts. I'd be forever seeing Gail across the street, or Ginger. I might try the Embankment or Covent Garden. There're a lot like me round Covent Garden. Or of course I could leave London altogether.

It's a free country, right?

The New Windmill Book of Stories Then and Now

Edited by Brian and Katherine Hawthorn

This anthology offers a rich selection of the best short stories by major authors from the nineteenth and twentieth centuries. The stories are arranged in thematic groups to help you compare the way people live, think, speak and write over time.

- In **Ghost Stories**, the characters in *The Red Room* by H G Wells and *Farthing House* by Susan Hill both find themselves in haunted rooms – with very different results!
- In **Fear**, all three stories, *The Whole Town's Sleeping* by Ray Bradbury, *A Terribly Strange Bed* by Wilkie Collins and *The Landlady* by Roald Dahl, will send shivers running up and down your spine . . .
- The stories in **Men and Women** explore the differences and similarities between the attitudes to women in *Tony Kytes, the Arch-Deceiver* by Thomas Hardy, *Seeing a Beauty Queen Home* by Bill Naughton and *Tickets, Please* by D H Lawrence.
- In **Murder Mysteries** you can compare the detectives in Roald Dahl's *Lamb to the Slaughter* with the greatest fictional detective of all time in Sir Arthur Conan Doyle's *The Speckled Band*.
- **Sacrifice** explores two stories in which the main characters make a huge sacrifice for the sake of their children: *The Son's Veto* by Thomas Hardy and *Survival* by John Wyndham

Age 14+
ISBN: 0 435 12482 X

Real People, Real Places
Edited by Angela Barrs

This is a rich and diverse selection of non-fiction written by a wide variety of people from a range of different cultures throughout the centuries. It includes: Autobiography, Letters, Diaries, Travel Writing and Journalism.

- In **Zlata's Diary** a young girl reveals the tragic waste of war as she writes about her daily experiences during the war in Sarajevo.
- In **A Long Walk to Freedom** Nelson Mandela writes about his part in the struggle to end apartheid in South Africa.
- In **Is That It?** Bob Geldof tells of his campaign to raise money to feed starving people in Africa.
- In **A Thousand Miles up the Nile** Amelia Edwards writes about her adventures as a female traveller at the end of the last century.

These are just some of the fascinating stories, insights and observations collected together in this book.

Age 13+
ISBN: 0 435 12448 X

Founding Editors: Anne and Ian Serraillier

Chinua Achebe Things Fall Apart
David Almond Skellig
Maya Angelou I Know Why the Caged Bird Sings
Margaret Atwood The Handmaid's Tale
Jane Austen Pride and Prejudice
Stan Barstow Joby: A Kind of Loving
Nina Bawden Carrie's War; The Finding; Humbug
Malorie Blackman Tell Me No Lies; Words Last Forever
Charlotte Brontë Jane Eyre
Emily Brontë Wuthering Heights
Melvin Burgess and Lee Hall Billy Elliot
Betsy Byars The Midnight Fox; The Pinballs; The Eighteenth Emergency
Victor Canning The Runaways
Sir Arthur Conan Doyle Sherlock Holmes Short Stories
Susan Cooper King of Shadows
Robert Cormier Heroes
Roald Dahl Danny; The Champion of the World; The Wonderful
Story of Henry Sugar; George's Marvellous Medicine; The Witches;
Boy; Going Solo; Matilda; My Year
Anita Desai The Village by the Sea
Charles Dickens A Christmas Carol; Great Expectations; A Charles
Dickens Selection
Berlie Doherty Granny was a Buffer Girl; Street Child
Roddy Doyle Paddy Clarke Ha Ha Ha
George Eliot Silas Marner
Anne Fine The Granny Project
Leon Garfield Six Shakespeare Stories
Ann Halam Dr Franklin's Island
Thomas Hardy The Withered Arm and Other Wessex Tales; The Mayor
of Casterbridge
Ernest Hemmingway The Old Man and the Sea; A Farewell to Arms
Barry Hines A Kestrel For A Knave
Nigel Hinton Buddy; Buddy's Song
Anne Holm I Am David

Janni Howker Badger on the Barge; The Nature of the Beast;
Martin Farrell
Pete Johnson The Protectors
Geraldine Kaye Comfort Herself
Daniel Keyes Flowers for Algernon
Dick King-Smith The Sheep-Pig
Elizabeth Laird Red Sky in the Morning
D H Lawrence The Fox and The Virgin and the Gypsy; Selected Tales
Harper Lee To Kill a Mockingbird
C Day Lewis The Otterbury Incident
Joan Linguard Across the Barricades
Penelope Lively The Ghost of Thomas Kemp
Geraldine McCaughrean Stories from Shakespeare; Pack of Lies
Bernard MacLaverty Cal; The Best of Bernard MacLaverty
Jan Mark Heathrow Nights
James Vance Marshall Walkabout
Ian McEwan The Daydreamer; A Child in Time
Michael Morpurgo The Wreck of the Zanzibar; Why the Whales Came;
Arthur, High King of Britain; Kensuke's Kingdom; From Hereabout Hill;
Robin of Sherwood
Beverley Naidoo No Turning Back; The Other Side of Truth
Bill Naughton The Goalkeeper's Revenge
New Windmill A Charles Dickens Selection
New Windmill Anthology of Challenging Texts: Thoughtlines
New Windmill Book of Classic Short Stories
New Windmill Book of Fiction and Non-fiction: Taking Off!
New Windmill Book of Greek Myths
New Windmill Book of Haunting Tales
New Windmill Book of Humorous Stories: Don't Make Me Laugh
New Windmill Book of Nineteenth Century Short Stories
New Windmill Book of Non-fiction: Get Real
New Windmill Book of Non-fiction: Real Lives, Real Times
New Windmill Book of Scottish Short Stories
New Windmill Book of Short Stories: Fast and Curious
New Windmill Book of Short Stories: From Beginning to End
New Windmill Book of Short Stories: Into the Unknown
New Windmill Book of Short Stories: Tales with a Twist
New Windmill Book of Short Stories: Trouble in Two Centuries
New Windmill Book of Short Stories: Ways with Words
New Windmill Book of Stories from Many Cultures and Traditions;
Fifty-Fifty Tuti-Fruity Chocolate Chip

How many have you read?